R.H. (Recep) Suleyman was born in London in 1990 just four days before Halloween, providing the foundation for great creativity. From an early age, his interest in writing was apparent, as he was continuously scribbling down the stories his mind would conjure up. Brought up on the many different fairy tales his grandparents would tell him, Recep's imagination was to become his greatest asset. His passion for writing flourished throughout his youth and he has often found it difficult to keep his imagination contained. Growing up in a large family, with many colourful cousins, aunts and uncles, has provided endless streams of inspiration.

With his writing, Recep aims to widen the imagination of the younger generation and offer some of the inspiration he was so fortunate to grow up with. His stories are not only for kids, though, as he hopes to remind older generations just how wondrous an enchanting tale can be.

D0683186

Tales Within

R.H. SULEYMAN

To
halil abi
hope you enjoy the
book

SilverWood

Published in paperback by SilverWood Books 2012

www.silverwoodbooks.co.uk

Copyright © R.H. Suleyman 2012

The right of R.H. Suleyman to be identified as the author of this work

has been asserted by him in accordance with the Copyright,

Designs and Patents Act 1988.

All rights reserved. No part of this publication may be reproduced,

stored in a retrieval system, or transmitted in any form or by any means,

electronic, mechanical, photocopying, recording or otherwise,

without prior permission of the copyright holder.

ISBN 978-1-78132-002-0

British Library Cataloguing in Publication Data

A CIP catalogue record for this book is available from the British Library

Set in Baskerville BT by SilverWood Books

Printed on paper sourced responsibly

This book is dedicated to my aunt, Ayse Bagan.
Her love of books never seemed to end.
May she rest in peace.

Contents

Introduction

Within the Victorian streets of London, there was once the most magnificent gift shop in the whole of England: the famous Snow Globe Shop. The shop sold the most beautiful snow globes in the entire country. Many people came from around the world to buy one of these magnificent hand-crafted objects, each made by a little old man. There were small globes, medium globes and some globes as big as your head, each one made with exquisite detail and craftsmanship. One could not walk past the shop without stopping to stare at these beautiful snow globes. Some said that the little old man possessed magical powers. However, what many did not know was that he was in truth a centuries-old wizard.

Within the shop, behind the third shelf to the right, there was a secret. The old man kept it well hidden. There was a secret passage way which opened once you twisted the red snow globe on the top shelf to the far right. The passageway led to a huge chamber full of thousands of snow globes.

Now these snow globes where nothing like the ones sold at the shop. These were magical. The snow globes on these shelves were actually prisons, which the little old man used to trap evil spirits, witches, wizards and demons. He created an individual domain within each snow globe where he locked them up far away from the world, so they would not spread their evil.

Right at the end of the huge chamber stood a tall Victorian glass cabinet with twenty snow globes upon each shelf. These were not prisons like the other globes in the chamber, but each of these snow globes told a tale... a tale of things that happened many, many years ago... in faraway lands... where animals could talk and magic was real...

Few people but the old man knew the tales trapped within those gleaming, glittering globes.

But draw closer... listen well. For now is the time to reveal those tales.

These are the Tales Within.

The Slave Donkey

nce upon a time, far across the seas in a land very different to ours, there lived a young donkey. He was an adventurous donkey at heart and had many adventures deep within the forest, for he enjoyed exploring and seeing the magnificent wonders of nature which lay there.

One bright and early morning, the donkey woke up by the lake within the forest and took a drink from it. He noticed many colours above in the sky and asked one of the birds what the colours in the sky were, for he had never seen anything like it. A bird replied that it was a rainbow. The donkey studied the curve of the rainbow, and decided that it looked as if the colours were falling to earth. The donkey was intrigued by this and decided to find out where the colours had fallen. So he began to follow the colours in the sky to find where it ended, but for as long as he walked he could not find where the colours had fallen. He walked for hours and when he looked up again at the sky, the colours had vanished. The donkey was upset that he could not find where the colours fell. He decided he would search for them tomorrow, for he was not quite ready to give up but was quite tired after all the walking he had done that day.

However the next morning, as the donkey went off into the forest for another adventurous day of finding where the colours of the rainbow fell, he was captured by a man from the village. The man enslaved him to do the chores within his farm. The donkey became sad and heartbroken, for he could no longer explore and have wild adventures within the forest, where he truly belonged. The donkey tried many times to escape, but the man was clever and always managed to find the poor donkey, and punished him for trying to escape. The donkey, fearing that he would be punished, decided never to try escape again.

One day in the village, as the donkey was forced to carry the heavy loads of man, he set his eyes upon a magnificent white horse. He saw the horse in all its glory – and saw too how the horse's rider respected him, treating him like a friend. The donkey knew from that day on that he wanted to be a horse, and so he rolled around in white chalk to become as white and beautiful as the horse. But the chalk dust made him sneeze, and when all the birds saw how silly he looked as he kept sneezing they began to laugh at him. The donkey was very much upset, for he knew he could never look as magnificent as the horse, even if he tried as hard as he could. The poor donkey, feeling

lost in what else to do, gave up all hope.

Then the day came where the donkey's owner died, and he was put on sale within the village. Many villagers looked at the heart-broken donkey lying on the floor, pretty much lifeless, as no one wanted to buy him.

He sat at the market for weeks and weeks, until the day came where a young boy saw the poor donkey. Feeling sorry for him, the boy went up to the donkey and began to stroke it. The donkey looked up and to his amazement saw how the child looked at him, as his equal – a friend, and not a slave. It brought hope to the donkey's broken heart and so he sprung back up, and as he did he knew he did not look like a horse, but he very much felt like one. The boy pleaded with his father to buy the donkey and so the father agreed. They took the donkey to their humble cottage, where the boy and the donkey soon became very close friends. They enjoyed exploring the forest together, looking for where the colours fell from the rainbow, for it fascinated both the child and the donkey. For many years they both had magnificent adventures together and the donkey knew exactly what it was like to be a horse, for that is what the boy made him feel like at heart, and the two lived happily ever after.

Princess in the Painting

n ancient times in a faraway land there lived a young thief. He was known to steal gold from the rich, and was eventually captured by the soldiers of the Kingdom and sentenced to death. As the thief waited in the dark, gloomy cell to be executed, a sorcerer appeared from the shadows, standing tall with coal black robes and messy grey-and-black hair.

The sorcerer said to the young thief, "I can save you and make you rich, Thief, but you must swear to become my servant until I no longer need your services." And the young thief agreed without a second thought, for this was his only way to escape.

So the sorcerer saved the thief from the cell and bought him to his dark castle. He ordered him to kidnap a beautiful princess from her tower within the Kingdom's palace and bring her to the sorcerer's castle.

So that is what the young thief did, for he had to obey everything the sorcerer said. Like a shadow he crept into the palace, not making a sound, and took the princess while she was fast asleep and bought her back to the sorcerer's dark castle.

When the sorcerer set eyes upon the beautiful princess, he let out a most evil and terrifying laugh, and began to sway his hands side to side, as he chanted:

Side to side, I sway my hands, one with such beauty I see upon my land, I call upon nature's ways, to forever hold her beauty in this place. One... two... three... let the colours of paint be, give them life to take one's life within a painting like thee.

14

He clapped his hands together, and with a flash of colourful bright lights the princess was trapped within a painting. The sorcerer ordered the thief to guard the painting with his life, and so he did.

As the days went by the thief noticed a locked chest, which was the first thing the sorcerer would look upon as he entered the castle, always making sure it was there. The thief could not help but wonder what was within the locked chest, and thought it must be something very valuable and of great importance. So one day he tried to open the chest but the sorcerer caught him and was furious.

The thief tried to placate the sorcerer. "I meant no harm, Master," he said. "I was simply curious."

But the sorcerer was outraged. "How dare you try to open the chest. Don't you know that curiosity killed the cat? Never try to open that chest – or any other – again. Never! Just guard the painting of the princess!"

And so that is what the thief did, for he was very afraid of the sorcerer.

As time passed the young thief guarded the painting of the princess. The princess, although still in the painting, was able to talk to the thief. She asked him to tell her all about himself and his life. At first the thief was shy, but she spoke gently to him and told him something of her own life and after a time he began to tell her of his own past.

It didn't matter how different they were or how different their families where. They had so much in common, and so as the days and months went by the thief and princess slowly began to fall in love. The evil sorcerer noticed the thief's feelings for the princess and saw this as a threat, so he told the thief a terrible lie. "She doesn't really love you, you young fool," he said. "She's using you so that you will set her free! As if a princess would fall in love with someone like you... a lowly thief!"

"No," protested the thief.

15

"Yes," said the sorcerer. "Look at yourself. Look in the mirror!" He waved a hand and a mirror appeared by magic. "Look now, you young fool and tell me what you see."

The thief glanced at himself, seeing the reflection of his ragged clothes. He stared for a long time at the skinny ragged reflection and soon he agreed with the evil sorcerer, for how *could* a princess fall in love with him? She deserved a prince charming.

From that day on the thief began to cover the painting up with a white sheet as he guarded it. The princess pleaded with him to talk to her, asking what the matter was.

"Have I said something to hurt you?" she asked.

But the thief would not answer. He stood guard, his back to the painting which was covered by a white sheet.

One morning the sorcerer prepared to leave the castle on one of his evil quests that would take him far, far away. He told the thief that he would be away for a couple of days and to keep an eye upon the Princess. The thief watched him go, feeling glad in his heart because he was so afraid of the sorcerer. He guarded the princess, but as the days past he became bored with no one to talk to. He remembered the sorcerer's chest and, after a while curiosity took control. The thief went to take a look at what was inside. He found the key and opened the chest to find within it a painting of a beating heart. The thief knew it must be the sorcerer's heart, and he had trapped it within the painting to grant him immortal life. The thief was very much intrigued, but then fear came rushing up his body. What if the sorcerer found out that he had opened the chest – what would he do to him? Fear gripped him as he remembered what the sorcerer had said. "Curiosity killed the cat". Could his curiosity *kill* him? He quickly sealed the chest shut and hoped the sorcerer would never find out that he had opened it.

That night the thief decided to walk to the nearby

village where there was a tavern. He was lonely with no one to talk to, and he knew the villagers would be good company. He was right – the villagers were cheerful and welcoming, and soon he was sitting at the bar drinking a flagon of ale. Suddenly a woman ran into the tavern, shouting, "Fire! Fire! Up at the sorcerer's castle!"

The thief, fearing for the life of the princess, ran out of the tavern and jumped onto a horse. He went riding as fast as the horse could take him to the dark castle. When he got there he jumped off the horse and ran into the raging flames of the castle, not thinking twice about his own life. He picked up the painting of the princess, who was screaming her heart out for someone to save her. The thief quickly ran out of the castle just as it came crumbling down.

Rocks and stones rained around the thief. Heat billowed from the flames. He ran faster, realising that the castle was falling down. As it did so the painting of the princess began to brightly glow. The frame became so hot that the thief could no longer hold it. He set it down... and from within the painting walked the beautiful princess.

The thief knew instantly that the spell upon her had been broken, for the fire had destroyed the painting of the evil sorcerer's heart. In turn the evil sorcerer was vanquished, never to harm anyone again.

The thief, unable to even look at the princess, told her that she was free and could go back to her beautiful palace and marry her prince charming. The princess smiled at the thief. "But you are my Prince Charming," she said.

"But I'm just a lowly thief dressed in rags," protested the thief.

"But you're not a thief," said the princess. "Not any more. You haven't stolen anything for many years." And then she told him that it didn't matter that he was dressed in rags, and nor did it matter how different their families were, or where they had been bought up, for she had fallen in love with him, and love didn't care about those things. Love was more important than where a person came from.

The thief looked up into the princess's glittering eyes and smiled. Soon after, the two were married in the castle with a magnificent feast in honour of the couple who lived happily ever after.

The Golden Curse

nce upon a time, long ago on the dark blue seas, there sailed a pirate ship called the Golden Snatcher. Its name was feared among all the sailors and even among other pirates for Captain Gold Tooth, the captain of the ship, hungered for gold like no other man. He would do anything for gold, and his lust for it was the only thing that the pirate captain could think of.

One stormy night the crew of the *Golden Snatcher* spotted a beautiful woman floating lifelessly within the waters. After dragging her on board the ship, Captain Gold Tooth was instantly struck by her beauty. Taking her to his cabin, he cared for her day and night and she soon was well again, and afterwards the two fell madly in love with each other. As time passed she gave him a child, a baby girl.

But things were soon to change and the captain's lust for gold became stronger, for now he used the excuse that he was doing it for his daughter and wife, so they could have a rich future. The woman, furious to see the pirate's lust for gold was yet again revived, jumped into the calm, blue sea. The captain, horrified by this, was about to jump in to save her, when suddenly the entire sea began to bubble as if it were boiling water and out burst the woman, standing high and mighty, even bigger than a sea serpent. In fact, she was seven times bigger than their own ship. And as she looked down upon them this is what she said, with her powerful voice that echoed over the sea:

My name is Calypso, goddess of the sea, and I have watched you for many years, Captain Gold Tooth, you and your lust for gold. I came to test you, to see whether love could change your ways, but I see that it hasn't and never will. So I shall curse you and your crew to roam the sea for all eternity. But there is a caution to this curse – for if you try to step on to land ever again, you shall turn into what you have lusted for all your life: gold! Let me tell you pirates that as with every curse, there is a way to break this curse, but I shall let you dig into your heart to find out what that might be, Captain Gold Tooth.

And with that she dived into the sea and vanished deep beneath the waves.

Years passed – hundreds of years, for the sea goddess had cursed them for all eternity. Yet the captain did not dig deep into his heart to find out how to end the curse. Instead he took the curse as a blessing of immortality and wreaked havoc among the sea and was feared within all the lands, along with his ship and his crew. They became known as the Bloody Immortals and that is exactly what they were, immortals that roamed the sea only for one purpose, to cause destruction and bloodshed just for their lust of gold. But there was one crew member that was nothing like the captain or the crew, and she was the captain's daughter, who had been given to him by the sea goddess Calypso those many years ago. The captain loved his daughter very much, but she was not happy upon the ship, as she always dreamt of stepping foot onto land. That is all she ever dreamt of, but she was told by her father that it could never happen, for if she ever tried to step on land she would be turned into solid gold.

One bright sunny morning the girl was woken up by canon fire. Rushing towards the top deck she saw a ship sailing behind a huge rock, the only ship to have not been sunk by the *Golden Snatcher*. It was then that she set eyes upon the young captain of the ship, and as the young captain saw her, the winds made her beautiful golden-brown hair sway from side to side. The two were instantly taken by each other. Captain Gold Tooth was furious that this ship was the first ship ever to escape being sunk by the *Golden Snatcher*. Captain Gold Tooth furiously shouted at his entire crew to set sail towards the rock, which the ship had hidden behind.

"No, Captain," protested the crew. "It could be a trap!"

But the captain shouted that they were immortals and that nothing could stop him from taking the gold and sinking the ship to the bottom of the sea.

So they set sail towards the rock, but as they sailed behind it they were shocked to find no sign of the ship. Captain Gold Tooth, burning up with anger, demanded that they find that ship, but before he could even finish what he was saying a canon went flying into the side of their ship and they began to shake as hundreds of canons blasted into it.

The girl, afraid and not knowing what to do, suddenly remembered what she felt when she looked upon the young captain of that ship. What if he were killed in this fighting? She could not bear that. She scrambled up into the ship's rigging in the midst of all the flying cannonballs and shouted at the crew of both ships to stop their firing, but no one listened to her. She kept shouting and shouting until her voice grew hoarse. How could she save the young captain, she wondered. Suddenly a power seemed to seethe through her. Her eyes began to glow a dark blue and as she shouted "Stop!" for the last time, the sea boiled up and a gush of water knocked the enemy ship upside down.

She watched in horror as all the men quickly swam towards land, but there was no sign of the young captain. Was he drowning? She knew in her heart that he must have

sunk beneath the waves, so she jumped into the sea to save him. She swam deep into the ocean and spotted him trapped between two barrels within the ship. She quickly dragged him out, and as they swam up, a bright light flashed and told her that the curse had been broken, and that she may step on to land. The girl pulled the captain on to the shore, and as she stepped upon the ground for the first time and felt her toes digging into the sand, she was amazed to find that she was still alive.

The captain opened his eyes and as their eyes met they both knew that they were destined to be with each other from that moment on.

"Is this what love feels like?" asked the girl.

The young captain nodded. "It must be," he said. "I have never felt this before."

Captain Gold Tooth and his crew, seeing the girl on land, could not believe their eyes and all shouted and cheered, "The curse is broken!"

They jumped into the sea with excitement, began to swim towards the shore and crawled onto the sand after hundreds of years of life on the seas. But suddenly the sands of the land grabbed hold of all the crew's feet and Captain Gold Tooth's too, and they could not move, as much as they struggled to. The sea began to boil up and glow, and as it did out walked Calypso.

Looking at her daughter she said, "Well done, my

dear, you have broken the curse for yourself, with your self-sacrifice to save a man you barely knew."

She then turned to Captain Gold Tooth and said, "As for you, Captain Gold Tooth... you and your crew have never known the true meaning of sacrifice or love. Nothing matters to you but gold. I see now that you will never change."

The sea goddess Calypso raised her hand. With a click of her fingers, the crew and Captain Gold Tooth screamed for the last time and slowly turned to solid gold.

The girl and young captain soon got married, never to set sail on the ocean ever again, and lived happily ever after.

The Wolf King

nce upon a time in a faraway land there lived a brave and powerful King, and when his son was born the land rejoiced. But the King was heartbroken, for his beloved Queen had died as she gave birth to the baby. One night the King, not wanting to even set eyes upon his son, took the new-born child deep into the woods and left him there upon a rock for the wolves to feed on.

As the full moon shone brightly upon the Kingdom and the forest, a mother wolf went to hunt for food for her cubs. She caught a deer and took it back for them, but when she reached home she was horrified to find her cubs had been eaten by a Big Bad Grizzly Bear. The mother wolf was distraught. She ran deep into the woods to kill the bear, but she could not find it. Instead, she heard a pitiful crying sound. She followed the sound of the cries to the rock, where she set eyes upon the baby. Immediately she felt sorry for him as he cried. She knew at once that he was hungry. She took the baby to her cave and fed it some of her wolf-milk. The crying stopped and as the baby fell fast asleep, the mother wolf watched the baby. She thought about how strange he looked... not like a wolf cub at all. He had no fur. And his snout was very short. And he cried instead of howling. But something about him eased the pain in her heart for her own dead cubs, and so she decided to look after the human baby.

Meanwhile, back in the heart of the Kingdom, the old King had been overthrown by a Dark Wizard, who was once the King's most trusted adviser. In fact, he was the one who had advised the King to get rid of the child that he could not bear to look upon. "Oh, your Royal Highness is heartbroken," he had said. "For your dear wife the Queen is dead. Never will your heart mend while the cause of her death – this child – is here in your Royal presence. You must rid yourself of the terrible reminder and get rid of the child." And he clasped his hands behind his back, his fingers crossed that the King would do as he said, for the Dark Wizard knew he could never overthrow the King while the child lived. And besides, long ago, a prophecy had foretold that the son of the King would be the one to destroy him. The Dark Wizard knew the child was a threat in all ways, so he had urged the King to be rid of him. And so the way was clear for him to overthrow the King and take charge of the Kingdom.

Meanwhile, back in the forest Mother Wolf cared for the child just like she would care for her own cubs. He grew fast and strong. She taught him to hunt and schooled him in the ways of the forest. As the years went by the child grew up to be an amazing hunter. The Mother Wolf would always tell her child to be careful as he went hunting in the forest and to be aware of the Big, Bad, Grizzly Bear, because she feared the same fate awaited him just like her baby cubs.

Upon the child's fifteenth birthday, the Mother Wolf gave him a sword that she found in the forest long ago, and as the Boy held the sword, he felt mighty and unstoppable. So that day he ran deep into the forest, looking forward to finding the Big, Bad, Grizzly Bear, and after searching for hours and hours, he found it by the river. At first when he set eyes upon the Big, Bad, Grizzly Bear a sense of fear made the Boy take a step back, but gripping the sword even tighter he charged towards the Big, Bad, Grizzly Bear and a ferocious fight took place. The Big, Bad, Grizzly Bear fought back, furiously growling at the Boy as it swung about its huge paws, but the Boy, acting quickly, swung his blade, swiftly cutting the bear's paws off. As the Big, Bad, Grizzly Bear howled in pain and agony, another swift swing of the Boy's sword cut the bear's head off. The Boy, proud of himself, took a look at his sword and smiled. He then dragged the bear's body across to woods and bought it back to Mother Wolf. She was so proud of her son that she made a coat for him from the bear's fur. That way the forest animals would know that he had killed the bear and could see how brave he was.

Back at the Kingdom, the Dark Wizard King had found a beautiful Maiden to marry, but the Maiden was afraid to even be in his presence. One night she wished upon a star, praying that the Dark Wizard King's evil reign would be over and to save her from this unholy marriage. Suddenly, a ball of white light came flying into her bedroom and the light began to glow brighter and brighter, revealing a beautiful fairy dressed in an enchanting white, glittery dress. She said to the young Maiden that she was her fairy godmother, and that it was only the Maiden who could end the reign of the Dark Wizard King. She had to find the real King – a young man who was not aware of his royal bloodline, and who was living within the forest amongst the animals themselves.

As the fairy godmother vanished with a flash of light the beautiful Maiden, not thinking twice about her own safety, tied her bedsheets together to make a rope and lowered herself out of the castle window. She ran away deep into the forest to find the real King.

Meanwhile back at the castle, the Dark Wizard King was told by one of his soldiers that his bride-to-be had run away. His face grew black with rage and he roared at his soldiers: "Find her! And bring her back to me alive or dead."

The next morning as the Boy went hunting in the woods, he spotted the beautiful Maiden hiding behind a tree. He slowly walked towards her, mesmerised by her beauty. He reached her side and tried to sniff her, for that was how wolves found out about the world. But when the Maiden turned around to see him staring and sniffing at her she let out a loud scream, for she saw a Wolf Boy clad in bear fur, his hair matted and his face filthy. She pushed him to the floor. As he fell, the Wolf Boy growled and twisted nimbly and quickly pushed himself up. The Maiden tried to speak to him, but he could not speak her human language, for he only knew how to speak the language of the wolves. Instead, he began to bark at her.

The Maiden was a little scared and pleaded with him to stop. He tilted his head to one side, trying to understand what she was saying. "Please," she said. "Don't bark any more. I won't hurt you."

Then suddenly, out from the bushes, jumped soldiers of the Dark Wizard King. They had been looking for the Maiden and when they heard her speak they had come quickly to capture her. The Wolf Boy quickly drew his sword and like a wild animal set about the soldiers. They were cowards, so when they were faced with this wild howling Wolf Boy they ran away deep into the forest.

Meanwhile, the beautiful Maiden had remembered what her fairy godmother had told her. She knew that this must be the real King – the young man who was not aware of his royal bloodline who had become part of the forest.

The Maiden walked with the Wolf Boy back to his cave. When the Mother Wolf set eyes on her, she viciously growled but the Wolf Boy barked at the Mother Wolf, telling her that the Maiden was harmless. So the Mother Wolf moved aside from the cave's entrance and invited her in. The Maiden decided that she would live within their cave and teach the Wolf Boy to read and write and speak – he was destined to be King, after all and he must be able to speak with his people.

The Maiden lived among the wolves for a year. She

slowly but steadily taught the Wolf Boy about the ways of humans. Soon he could speak… and read… and write. They talked for hours about the ways of the forest and also about the world of humans. They grew close and then one day the Maiden saw the Wolf Boy press his hand to his heart. He looked at her and then she pressed her hand to her own heart – and they knew that they were falling in love.

The two had so much fun within the forest. But the Maiden always knew that the Wolf Boy was the future King and it was her duty to help him claim the Kingdom back when he was truly ready. One night she decided that she would tell him his true identity, and as the two laid upon the grass gazing at the stars, the Maiden said to him that she had something she had wanted to tell him for a long time about his true destiny.

The Wolf Boy was intrigued. "What is it?" he asked.

But before she could tell him, the Dark Wizard's soldiers sneaked up behind the two and captured them. They tied their hands and threw them roughly into a wagon and soon they were on their way to the castle of the Dark Wizard King. As they travelled the Maiden told the Wolf Boy everything she could about his true identity and his destiny to be King.

The Wolf Boy looked up at the full moon and began to howl at it. He howled and howled and howled, and as his howling echoed throughout the forest and the Kingdom, other wolves began to look up at the moon and howl back. The howling spread and soon all the wolves in the entire Kingdom and forest were gazing up at the moon and howling.

The Maiden asked him what he had done, and the Wolf Boy told her that he had raised an army. An army of wolves! Even now the army was making its way towards the castle, for the Wolf Boy was ready to claim back what was rightfully his.

The Wolf Boy and the Maiden were taken to the Dark

Wizard King's chambers, and as the Dark Wizard set his eyes upon the Maiden, he angrily demanded that she tell him why she had run away. The Maiden shook with fear as she told him that she did not love him and that she would never marry him. The Dark Wizard King let out a most evil and sinister laugh. Running his fingers up and down his staff he told her that he was all-powerful and that he would *make* her marry him.

Meanwhile a huge army of wolves gathered outside the castle and began to howl at the moon as they awaited their King's command. The howling echoed around the castle walls and the soldiers of the castle began to shake in fear. The Wolf Boy looked at the Dark Wizard King, and for the first time in his life the Dark Wizard felt afraid. Who was this boy, he wondered, clad in black bearskin?

"Give me back my Kingdom," the Wolf Boy said.

At that moment the Dark Wizard knew that the boy was the old King's son and he began to tremble, for he remembered the prophecy that foretold his doom. Then the Wolf Boy howled and as he did the army of wolves began to attack the castle's soldiers. The Dark Wizard, acting swiftly, summoned a gust of wind from his staff and the Maiden and Wolf Boy went flying across the great hall.

"He's escaping!" cried the Maiden as the Dark Wizard King fled from the chamber. He ran down the spiralling staircase but at the bottom of it awaited Mother Wolf.

The Mother Wolf knew that this man was like the Big Bad Grizzly Bear who had killed her cubs all those years ago. He meant harm to her Wolf Boy, but she would not allow it. She took the Dark Wizard King's staff in her fierce jaws and tossed it out of a nearby window.

The Dark Wizard King screamed with great rage, and taking out his sword was about to strike down the Mother Wolf, when the Boy pounced on him, and pushed him out of the window.

There was a moment of silence – and then with a cry the Dark Wizard King plunged to his death. The soldiers that had been loyal to him ran away, while those who had served the old King cheered and swore allegiance to the Wolf Boy.

From that day on the Wolf Boy became known as the Wolf King and ruled all the lands, respecting all his people and animals. He married the beautiful Maiden, and they lived happily ever after.

The Lonely Rose

ong ago when the world was young, there lived a beautiful Princess who was famed for her beauty among the lands. An evil old witch, jealous of the Princess's looks and knowing she herself could never be as attractive, cast a evil curse upon the Princess, turning her into a rose. She was the most exquisite, fiery-red rose you would ever set eyes upon, but she was a lonely rose, isolated from all the other flowers as she stood alone among the grass. Throughout the summer, she bloomed so beautifully, but as autumn began to get closer the rose started to fall desperately ill. Luckily, a little old lady saw the rose and even though its colour had begun to fade, she knew that she could make the rose bloom beautifully again. Slowly digging it out of the earth and trying not to damage the beautiful rose, the old lady placed it in a flower pot and took it to her cottage.

She cared for the rose day and night, watering and tending to it, and when the winter came she placed the rose near the fire to assure that it would not get cold, but not too near in case it got too hot. When the summer came again the rose blossomed with such beauty. However, the rose was still very lonely, even though it did have the company of the old lady, who would sit and talk to the flower, even though it could not talk back. The rose wished very much for a prince charming to come along and save her from this awful curse. She waited and waited for many years, but it was still just her and the old, caring lady.

One beautiful night a Fairy Prince flew into the cottage looking for some food, but when he saw the beautiful rose

he decided to steal it, and so he did. The Fairy Prince took the rose back to Fairy Land, which was under a huge, magnificent tree within the forest, and once all the fairies set eyes upon the rose, they all fell in love with its magnificent beauty. When the fairy elder saw it, he knew instantly that this was no ordinary rose, but in fact a princess who had been cursed into the form of a rose. All the fairies were very much intrigued and asked how they could break the curse and free the Princess. The elder fairy told them that if someone loved her – not for her beauty but for her heart – then and then only would the curse be broken.

So all the fairy princes began to fly to the beautiful rose and one by one told her their deepest darkest secrets, hoping that this somehow showed that they loved her and not her beauty, but it seemed not to work. That night all the princes went to sleep trying to figure out a way to break the curse.

As all the fairy princes laid in their beds thinking of the beautiful rose, a young blind fairy, the cleaner of the realm, entered the fairy hall where the rose stood blooming with beauty. The young blind fairy began to clean. When he accidentally bumped into the rose, he couldn't see it but he could feel the rose's heart, so he began to talk to it. Suddenly the rose was granted lips, and so it began to talk back.

The two talked and talked for hours and hours. The young blind fairy cleaner grew tired and went in to kiss the beautiful rose goodnight. As he did, with a bright flash of red light, the spell was broken. The beautiful Princess was transformed into a fairy herself, and she married the young blind fairy, and they lived happily ever after.

The White Lamp

nce upon a time, a very long time ago across the oceans, there lived a selfish and lustful king, who abused his kind queen and never paid much attention to his only son. The Kingdom called him King John the Selfish. One day, the Queen fell desperately ill and passed away soon after. The entire Kingdom mourned her death except the King, who a few days later ordered a huge ball to be arranged – with music and dancing and tables full of wonderful food. He said that they must invite all the beautiful maidens of the land, for he was seeking a new queen. The entire Kingdom was in shock at how cold-hearted the King truly was. But nobody was in more shock and absolute devastation than the poor young Prince William.

However, the ball still went ahead despite the entire Kingdoms' disapproval. Many young and beautiful maidens travelled from across the lands to seek the King's hand in marriage. As the palace filled with music and dancing and laughter, the King kept a watchful eye for his new queen.

The poor Prince just sat in the corner of the lavishly decorated hall, remembering his dear, sweet mother. Then suddenly the music stopped when a beautiful maiden far from across the seas entered the hall. Everyone in the hall stopped to take a glimpse of the wondrous beauty she possessed – hair as golden as the burning sun, eyes that sparkled in the moonlight, and beautiful skin as white as snow. As the Prince looked up and set eyes upon her, his heart felt like it was about to burst right out of his chest and when the beautiful Princess set eyes upon the young, handsome Prince, she smiled a most angelic smile.

The King watched in a rage of jealousy as the two instantly fell in love. He was furious, for he wanted to marry the most beautiful maiden, and she was definitely the most beautiful maiden he had ever set eyes upon, but he could see his son had won her heart. The King angrily stood up and called his guards to arrest his son and lock him up in the tower. The Princess pleaded for an answer to this cruel behaviour, but the King simply stated that his son had betrayed him. Poor Prince William was locked up in the dirtiest and darkest dungeon cell within the tower.

The King tried to win the beautiful Princess's love, but she was already very much in love with Prince William. She secretly visited him every morning, which gave the poor Prince something to hope for. The King, learning of the Princess's secret visits, became consumed with anger. "If I cannot not have the beautiful Princess," he declared. "Then nobody shall!"

And so he banished the Princess to a castle on a deserted island. No one in the land knew where she was except the King. As his morning visits from the Princess stopped, William began to lose hope, thinking she must have moved on and found a new prince to love.

An Enchantress, seeing the cruelty that the King had committed upon the young Prince and beautiful Princess, cast a curse upon the selfish and cruel King. Not only would he never be able to love a beautiful maiden ever again, but the Enchantress formed a hideously revolting scar upon the King's face, so that – with a single touch from him – beautiful maidens would receive the same scar upon their own faces. Soon, every beautiful maiden feared the King and his curse. They all deserted the Kingdom and no beautiful maidens dared to set foot upon the cursed King's lands.

The King's loneliness made him turn into a bitter

old man with no happiness left inside him, only rage and indescribable anger. He became worse than a hungry beast.

The beautiful Princess, locked up within her castle, began to grow desperately ill, for without her Prince she felt like there was nothing to live for. What she did not know was that she was a prisoner upon an enchanted island. The beautiful flowers of the island saw this and could not bear to see such a beautiful Princess grow desperately ill for her love. The enchanted flowers on the island cast a spell upon her to make her fall into a deep sleep, only to be awakened by the prince that she so desperately desired.

The flowers called upon the help of a trusty mouse called Cedric. They asked Cedric to go and find the Prince and bring him to awaken the beautiful Princess from her eternal sleep. Cedric excitedly agreed, for he loved a good adventure, and so he hopped onto his little boat and began to row to the cursed Kingdom of King John the Selfish.

Cedric rowed for many nights, overcoming terrible storms and huge waves. He was even attacked by a school of sharks but the brave little mouse would not give up, trusting his little boat and tiny blade as he carried on with his journey. Finally and at long last he made it to the cursed Kingdom. The mouse rushed through the busy streets and into the Prince's cell up in the huge tower, where the Prince was sitting, looking lost, with no hope of setting eyes upon his beautiful Princess ever again.

Cedric wriggled between the bars of the window and said, "Stop looking so down, Lord Prince, for I have come to take you to your Princess."

The Prince was astounded. "A mouse is speaking to me," he cried. "I have been alone for so long that I am going mad... I'm imagining things."

"No," said Cedric. "I really can talk."

But the Prince ignored him.

"Now look here, Prince William," Cedric said crossly.

"I've come a long way to help you." The mouse took out his little sword and demanded the Prince listen to him, for the Princess had fallen into an enchanted sleep and was waiting for him to awaken her.

The mouse quickly cut him loose from his chains.

The Prince stared in amazement. "Can it be true?" he asked, stretching out his hands, which were now free of the chains. The Prince's heart began to fill with hope for the first time in many years. He crept out of the dungeons with his trusted new friend, Cedric the mouse.

The Prince and the mouse set sail for the enchanted island where the Princess was locked away. But what they didn't know was that the King had seen the Prince escape, and he himself took a bunch of his strongest and cruellest soldiers and also set sail for the island.

As the Prince and the mouse sailed through the calm blue sea the Prince was very excited to think that he would soon be reunited with his beloved Princess once again. But soon he set eyes upon the King's ship which was gaining speed and catching up with them.

"We must row faster, Cedric!" he cried. But before he could even finish saying the mouse's name, a hideous sea monster suddenly burst out from under the sea. It let out a terrible screech. The Prince and mouse, fearing for their lives, began to row as quickly as they could. But to their horror the great waves the sea monster was creating with its enormous tail was pushing them towards a huge icy cliff. They tried to row away from it, but it was no use. Then a sudden burst of white light flashed upon them and the two vanished.

The King's eyes widened in surprise, for where had they gone? Now he and his men were left to face the terror and wrath of the sea monster.

The young Prince William and mouse woke up on the edge of the cliff, which was part of an enormous icy mountain. From the dripping waters within the mountain, chairs begin to magically form from the ice. A giggling, crazy old woman then appeared, and everything about her was completely white. She was dressed in white with messy white hair and white glowing eyes. She told the Prince and Cedric that she had bought them here herself, using her magic powers.

"Are you a witch?" the Prince asked.

The old woman began to laugh. She assured them that she was no witch, but an Enchantress of the sea and told the young Prince that she had been watching him and his cruel father for some time. She was the enchantress who cast the curse upon the King, and asked the Prince what he would do about his horrid father, King John the Selfish.

The Prince told her that they would run away, far away. The Enchantress seemed disappointed in his answer. "You cannot run all your life," she said. "You cannot run away from problems. No! You must solve them."

So she sat down to think of what they could do with King John the Selfish and it then came to her. With a cunning smile she stood up and asked the Prince if he was prepared to do anything for his love. The Prince stated yes, and so the Enchantress pointed at the river that ran through the icy mountain and from the waters she created a white lamp. Giggling with delight she told the Prince that this lamp was magical and because his father had been such a selfish king and thought of no one else but himself, there was only one punishment fit for him – to serve other people's needs, forever. She said that the Prince must give the lamp to the King and tell him to make a wish with it, and when he did he would be transformed into a genie and trapped within the lamp. There he would have to serve those that found the lamp and become their servant for all eternity.

"It is a fitting punishment for one who has been so selfish!" The Enchantress let out another delightful giggle, very proud of herself, and the Prince agreed to take the white lamp.

The Prince thanked the Enchantress, and from the waters that ran through the mountain she magically created a huge spiralling stairway which reached high up to the top. She then told the Prince and Cedric to walk up the stairway till they reached the very top, and that they would find themselves on the Princess's island.

Thanking the Enchantress again, they begin to walk up the spiralling stairway. After a very exhausting walk, up, hundreds of stairs, they came to a white door. They opened it and walked through, and the Prince at last set eyes upon the beautiful Princess lying asleep, covered in beautiful flowers. He was just about to hurry to her side when King John the Selfish appeared. Drawing his sword began to battle his own son.

Cedric knew he had to get help. The little mouse quickly ran out and asked the enchanted flowers for their help. The entire ground began to shake and from beneath the floor great strong vines burst through and entwined around the King until he could not move.

The Prince looked at his father struggling to break free, and knew this was his chance. "He held the lamp aloft. "Father... make a wish!" he said. "Just one wish, and it will come true."

"Why are you helping me?" asked the King.

"I'm not helping you, Father, but myself. Wish yourself out of my life and you never have to see me again."

The Prince handed the lamp to the King and the vines that held him loosened. The King stood up and shouted, "Fool! You think I will make that wish? No! Instead I shall wish that you never existed."

As he spoke, white smoke began to trickle out of the lamp and the King gave a sinister laugh, but he then noticed the smoke was gathering around him instead of

his son. He screamed, "No!" as he was sucked into the lamp, never to harm his son again.

The Prince slowly walked to where the Princess laid, leaned in and kissed her beautiful lips. She slowly opened her eyes as she awakened from her enchanted sleep, and the two lived happily ever after as king and queen of the land.

The Minotaur's Cave

nce upon a time, long ago in a faraway land there was a small village that lived in fear of the Minotaur within its cave. Many brave young soldiers went to kill the beast but never returned alive; many brave young soldiers even travelled from over the seas to kill the horrific beast, but once they entered the cave, they were never seen again. The villagers began to think the Minotaur was unbeatable and it would take a miracle to destroy it, so they agreed that no one was to enter the Minotaur's cave ever again.

One day a little girl went deep into the forest to pick some flowers and she heard someone crying. She began to look for who it was, and as she followed the sound of the crying, she got closer and closer to the Minotaur's cave. Forgetting the stories she had been told about the horrid beast that dwelled there, she entered it. As she walked deeper and deeper into the long, dark cave, she spotted the huge hideous beast whose body was that of a man but which had the head of a bull with huge, sharp horns and on the ends of its arms were great fists all sharp with wicked claws.

At first the girl was frightened, but then she realised that the Minotaur was crying. Feeling deeply sorry for the beast, she slowly moved forwards and began stroking its furry back.

"Why are you crying?" she asked.

"Everybody hates me," the Minotaur sobbed. "I'm fed up with being alone. No one comes here anymore. They're all afraid of me."

"I'm not afraid of you," the girl said.

The Minotaur lifted up his huge head and could not believe his eyes. A girl was standing there smiling at him and not trying to kill him or run away from him. The Minotaur smiled back and the little girl asked the Minotaur if he would like to be friends. The Minotaur very excitedly jumped into the air and said he would very much like that.

So from that day on the little girl would visit her new friend every day, bringing him some of the tasty apple and blueberry pies her mother made.

One day the little girl and the Minotaur went to explore the cave and she stayed a little longer than usual, so her mother began to worry. Eventually she went to look for her young daughter within the woods. When she came near the cave she saw her little girl's hair ribbon upon the floor. Terrified – and fearing the worst – she ran back to the village shouting hysterically that the Minotaur had taken her daughter.

The whole village gathered round that night and worried that it would happen to other children if the Minotaur had started to hunt outside his cave.

"We must do something!" cried the mothers of the village. "The beast must be stopped. We cannot allow it to take our children."

So the men of the village decided to kill the Minotaur. Gathering whatever weapons they could find, they all marched to the Minotaur's cave that dark, gloomy night to slay the beast.

Meanwhile, as the little girl and Minotaur explored the cave, the girl became tired and was finding it hard to keep her eyes open. The Minotaur told her that she could sleep there that night, and so she did, falling asleep upon his bed. The Minotaur decided to go and fetch some berries and water for when she woke up. But when he left the cave he found that outside was a huge mob waving weapons, shouting and roaring at the Minotaur, ready to attack. The Minotaur let out a ferocious roar trying to scare them away, but instead they all began to attack the Minotaur. Horrified, the beast tried to defend himself, knocking some of the men to the floor and tossing others across the forest.

The Minotaur fought bravely, trying not to seriously injure any of them so they would leave him be, but then the girl's father caught the beast by surprise and pierced it through the heart.

The Minotaur let out his last roar – a great echoing bellow which awakened the girl. She began to look for him in the cave, but when she realised he was nowhere to be seen she ran outside. There she found the Minotaur's body covered in blood. She fell upon the Minotaur's lifeless body and wept, crying aloud: "My friend! My friend!"

The girl's father, confused to see his daughter crying over the beast, came forward and tried to take her hand to lead her away.

"There's no need to cry," he said. "The beast is dead. He can't hurt you any more."

The girl took one look at her father and shouted: "He's no beast. He was my friend. *You* are the beast! You've killed my best friend." Turning her back on her father, she bent her head over the Minotaur's still body and wept harder. Her tears dropped bright upon the dead beast's head.

The Minotaur then suddenly began to glow brightly and the girl quickly got up and watched as the soul of the Minotaur left its body.

As it floated within the air it smiled at the little girl and said that she was his best friend too, and that after all the years when he was treated like a monster, she was the only one who understood him and saw him for who he really was inside. She had made him happy.

The soul of the Minotaur comforted the girl and told her not to worry, for he was going to a better place where there would be more like him.

"I will never forget you," he said.

And then, with a sudden flash of light, the Minotaur vanished.

The girl went on to live a long and happy life, and she too never forgot her best friend the Minotaur.

The Golden Apple

n another place and another time there lived a wicked enchantress who was obsessed with her own beauty and eternal life. Using all her dark magic she created an enchanted tree, which every ten years produced only two apples – the golden apple which would grant her youth and eternal life, and the white apple which stole ones youth away, turning them to stone. For the golden apple's magic to work she had to feed the white apple to a young child and drain its youth.

Our story begins within an isolated village in the woods, where there lived a young boy who was very mischievous. He would always go exploring in the forbidden forest and as much as his father and mother told him not to, he never listened. He did as he pleased, for he was a naughty boy.

One day when the boy went so deep into the forest he could not find his way back. Afraid and scared, he began to cry and kept shouting that he promised to never be naughty again.

Then he heard a little squeaky voice and it said to him, "Why would you ever want to be good? That is never fun. Being naughty is so much more fun."

When the boy looked up he could not believe his eyes, for kneeling on a branch in front of him was a tiny blue fairy. The fairy flapping its little wings flew into the boy's face and said, "Before you say anything, Boy, let me just make doubly sure that you do not mistake me for a fairy, for they are do-gooders and my worst enemies. I am in fact a *pixie* and pixies are mischievous and always up to no good. I hate fairies and their well-mannered behaviour so make sure you do not mistake me for one."

Delighted to have found someone so like himself, the boy nodded in agreement. The pixie, smiling delightfully, then asked the boy if he wanted to have some fun. With a big smile the boy quickly jumped to his feet and said, "Yes!"

The pixie, very much excited itself, began to flap its little wings faster than usual and told the boy that it was time to bring some mischief to the forest. Full of cunning, it rubbed together its tiny blue hands.

That day in the forest the boy and the pixie ran around causing all sorts of trouble to the poor animals there. They had so much fun swinging from tree to tree, plucking the feathers from the poor birds, stealing honey from the bees' nest, splashing water at the cats, riding on the deers' backs. All in all, it was a pretty mischievous day. As the sun set and the moon shone, the boy and the pixie fell fast asleep, very tired and proud of all the trouble they had caused.

The creatures of the forest hoped that this was just one day, and that the naughtiness and the torment would stop. But no. Every morning that followed the two would get up and plan new ways to cause trouble around the forest. The two had become very good friends and the boy had forgotten all about his family. The animals in the forest soon grew tired of all the trouble the two were causing and decided to do something about it.

That night the animals gathered around to decide what they would do. The cats said to make trouble for them and catch them at their own game, but the other animals agreed this would only make them wreak even more havoc. The badger suggested they kill them, but all the animals agreed that none of them could bring themselves to kill anyone, no matter how naughty they were. Then in walked the white wolf, and said they should tell the boy and the pixie about the evil Enchantress's castle not far from the forest.

All the animals were confused. "How will this help?" they asked.

"Simple," the wolf said. "If we tell that naughty pair about the castle, they are sure to want to explore it. And we all know that who ever goes into the castle never comes out again!"

And so the animals agreed that this was the only way.

While the boy and the pixie were stealing some honey as usual, the white wolf walked by and asked them if they wanted to do something really fun and mischievous. The two curiously asked what the wolf had in mind, and he told them about the Enchantress's castle not far from the forest. The boy and the pixie, intrigued by the idea of exploring an Enchantress's castle, decided that this was most definitely an adventure they wanted to have.

After travelling for many hours they soon set eyes upon the enormous castle and its huge black gates – the biggest gates they had ever seen. Their eyes widened with excitement. The pixie quickly flew over the gates, but the boy could not climb them for they were far too high. So the pixie grabbed hold of his friend and dragged him into the air and over the gates, dropping him on the other side. The boy fell right into thorn bushes, and started screaming and jumping up and down, trying to get the thorns out. The pixie could not stop laughing. Then suddenly the huge golden castle doors began to open, and the two quickly hid behind bushes worrying it might be the evil Enchantress. But there was no one in sight; it seemed the doors just magically opened by themselves. The two quickly ran in as the doors began to shut.

The boy and the pixie entered a very long and thin corridor with candles on either side lighting up the passage. The boy began to carefully walk down the huge red carpet that stretched down the entire corridor, taking every step with caution so the wooden floors beneath would not creak.

The pixie fluttered its wings gently so it too did not make a single sound. They then came to two doors at the end of the corridor. The boy tried the first one, but it was locked. He then tried the second one, and the door slowly creaked open to reveal another even longer corridor, which seemed endless, with many doors on each side.

The naughty friends excitedly walked in to explore. But as they tried all the doors they seemed to be tightly locked, until at long last one of the doors creaked open to reveal an enormous hall with many creepy paintings hanging upon the walls. The boy walked in, forgetting to shut the door behind him, for he was well and truly mesmerised by everything in the hall. The pixie thought he should shut the door before it slammed and alerted someone to their presence in the castle. Before the pixie could do so, however, a hand suddenly grabbed hold of its shoulder and the door slowly shut behind him.

Unaware of what was happening behind him, the boy gazed at the bizarre paintings upon the walls of dragons and hideous creatures of the night.

Then with a bright flash of light, a long table magically appeared in the middle of the great hall, lit with many candles. An old lady walked in with ugly, wrinkly old skin, long hideous nails and long grey hair. Her hair was so long that it dragged across the floor as she walked closer towards the table and sat down at the very far end. The boy slowly backed away with his heart pumping with fear, for he knew she must be the evil Enchantress.

"Don't be frightened," the Enchantress said.

But the boy kept slowly backing towards the door, which seemed miles away.

Then the Enchantress lifted up her hand with her skeleton-like thin fingers and gave them a click, and magically a magnificent feast appeared upon the table There was everything a hungry person could think of – chicken, pork chops, lamb, succulent vegetables and luscious fruit.

The boy was very hungry and stared in awe at the feast upon the table, licking his lips.

"It's all for you," the Enchantress told him. "Come... eat... do not be afraid."

However the boy remembered some of the things the villagers had said about her, and it frightened him to the core. "No," he whispered, his heart cold with fear.

The Enchantress leaned forward and comforted him with a soft voice. "There is nothing to fear," she said. "People have always misjudged me and made up horrible stories about me..." And with that she began to cry.

The boy, feeling sorry for her, decided to sit down.

The Enchantress slowly wiped away her tears and smiled. Clapping her hands together she said, "Let the feast begin!"

Out of nowhere magnificent dancers, jugglers, magicians and clowns appeared within the great hall. The boy laughed to see them, and then remembered his friend the pixie. He looked around, but the pixie was nowhere to be seen. He asked the Enchantress if she had seen his friend. The Enchantress told him that she had in fact seen the pixie going to explore some parts of the castle alone, for he no longer wanted to be friends with him.

The boy was hurt by this news and began to cry so the Enchantress got up and went beside him and putting her long, thin skeleton-like fingers upon his shoulders, told him not to worry, for he had a new friend now. This comforted the boy and so they carried on to enjoy the magnificent feast.

For two days the boy was looked after like a king by the Enchantress, who attended to his every need. All the while the poor pixie had been trapped within a cage, but finally – after much strife and struggle – the little creature managed to break out. It went flying around the castle as fast as its wings could carry it, looking for the boy. When at long last it found him within a bathroom having a hot bath alone, the pixie quickly told him that they had to leave, for the evil Enchantress knew that they were there.

The boy told him that the Enchantress was not evil and a very nice, kind old woman, and that she was his new friend. The pixie pleaded with him to understand that she was tricking him, but the boy angrily refused and insisted that the pixie go away.

"I am staying here with the Enchantress," he declared. "You and I are no longer friends!"

The pixie, hurt by the boy's words, left the room and went to look for a way out of the castle, comforting himself that he didn't need friends anyway. The pixie then heard the Enchantress talking to herself, so the pixie quietly looked through the keyhole to listen to what she was saying, and heard the most devilish plan she had for the boy. The pixie was horrified – fearing for the boy's life, he quickly flew back to the bathroom. But the boy was no longer there!

In a panic, the pixie began flying around the castle looking in every room he could find, but the boy was nowhere to be found. The pixie then remembered the Enchantress talking about an enchanted tree, so he started to look for the garden.

Meanwhile, the Enchantress and boy where walking through a magnificent maze within the garden, and when they came into the middle of the maze, there stood the enchanted tree, so tall that it looked like it was touching the sky. The Enchantress told the boy that the tree's apples were in fact wishing apples.

"Can I have one?" asked the boy, excited.

"Of course, my dear," said the Enchantress with a smile.

At a click of her fingers one of the branches of the tree bent down towards the boy. There was a white apple hanging upon the branch, so the boy picked it off. He polished it on his sleeve and held it up to the light. How it gleamed! How succulent it looked! How delicious it would taste. So sweet and juicy. He lowered the apple, brought it to his mouth, and slowly went to take a bite...

Suddenly – from nowhere – in flew the pixie and snatched the apple from him. The Enchantress screamed in anger and clicked her fingers together, making the pixie's wings shrivel and vanish. The pixie began to fall. He cried out, "Help me!"

The boy, fearing for the pixie's life, quickly reached out his arms to catch his friend.

"Don't eat the apple," the pixie said, "or you will turn to stone."

The boy stared, and then said slowly, "I believe you. You're my friend and friends trust each other."

Enraged, the Enchantress clicked her fingers again and a huge, hideous, white snake burst out from the ground. It slid towards them and opened its enormous fangs. The boy snatched up the apple and hurled it as hard and fast as he could. It went flying into the snake's mouth and the snake turned into stone.

The Enchantress's eyes burned red with anger and as she screamed and shouted. Thunder and lightning began to roar and as the two friends watched she slowly turned into stone, letting out her last evil scream.

"I'm so sorry," the boy said to the pixie. "I should never have trusted her. I should have believed you."

The pixie smiled at him and the two became even

better friends from that day on. They went to find the boy's village and when they did, he promised never to be naughty again. The boy's parents were filled with delight. Even the mischievous pixie vowed never to be naughty again and when he said this, with a bright flash of light he was transformed into a beautiful fairy and they lived happily ever after. And in the forest, the animals breathed a sigh of relief.

Hollow Tree

nce upon a time a long while ago, there lived a rich respected family. They had a beautiful four-year-old daughter, whom they loved very much, called Angelina. She was an adventurous young girl at heart, who loved to play around within their huge beautiful garden. However, things were soon to change.

One dreadful winter day her father fell desperately ill. Angelina was distraught to see her father in such pain and refused to leave her father's side. But every day her father seemed to get worse and the doctors had lost hope that he could be saved. Angelina refused to give up hope and always held tightly to her father's shaking hand.

One day, when he was lying exhausted on his pillows, her father began to tell Angelina her favourite fairy tale...

Underground within a huge hollow tree there was a beautiful village. The people who lived there were cats who worked day and night to keep their village as it should be...

Angelina listened intently to her beloved father's voice. However, that most awful moment had come. Her father slowly closed his eyes and went to sleep, never to wake up again.

One year passed and everyday Angelina thought of her father. She would get up early each morning and before doing anything else she would run to the garden, spend an hour or two looking for the most beautiful lily and place it on her father's bed. Another dreadful day came when her mother had to marry again so that they did not lose their beautiful home. However, the man she had married was cruel and cold-hearted, and as soon as he moved into their house he treated both Angelina and his mother like his servants. He made them cook, clean and farm, working day and night. One day when Angelina was dusting the living room she accidentally dropped a vase. It smashed upon the floor shattering into pieces. Her cruel stepfather ran into the room and began to beat her with his belt. He called her the most horrible names.

Angelina ran upstairs to her father's bed. She picked up the beautiful lily she had placed there and began to pray to her father to help them. As her tears began to drop upon the beautiful lily, a magnificent blue light shot out from within the flower and her father's spirit appeared to her.

"Father," she gasped. "Is that really you?"

"It is, my sweet daughter," the spirit said. "I cannot bear to see you living like this. You must run… run away into the woods and find the hollow tree."

"The h-h-hollow tree?"

"The one in the fairytale I used to tell you. It's real. You can find it if you look hard!"

And so Angelina ran as fast as her little legs could take her, deep into the forest. She then stopped under an enormous oak tree and fell to the muddy ground and began to weep. She wept until she could weep no more, and then she began to take notice of her surroundings. She could not believe what she saw. She quickly rubbed her eyes in disbelief and opened them again to see if it was still there but it was: a little wooden door within the side of the huge tree. She tried to turn the wooden doorknob but it seemed to be locked. She looked to see if there was a key lying around and as she lifted her head up, looking at the huge branches on the tree, she noticed something shining at the end of one of the branches. She looked at it carefully and saw that it was a key. Thinking it must be the key for the door, she tried to get up to the branch, but it was too high.

"Oh, what shall I do?" she asked herself. "This must be the hollow tree, and I must go inside if I'm to be safe."

Just then she heard a loud drilling noise. Looking around she saw a green woodpecker pecking at the tree. As she gazed at it, fascinated by what the bird was doing, it suddenly stopped pecking, looked at Angelina and asked her what she was looking at, muttering, "Can't a woodpecker peck in peace these days?"

Angelina was amazed that the woodpecker could speak. "Can you... she said hesitantly. "Can you fetch that key for me?"

"Perhaps," said the woodpecker. "Is it *your* key?"

Angelina replied with a stutter, "Y-y-yes."

The woodpecker, fluttering around thoughtfully, replied, "If you can repeat this phrase, three times and only three times without a single stutter, then I shall believe the key is yours and fetch you the key, do we have a deal?"

Angelina nervously nodded.

"Now listen carefully as I shall only say it once," said the woodpecker. "How much wood could a woodpecker peck if a woodpecker could peck wood?"

Angelina took a deep breath and repeated the phrase. "How much wood could a woodpecker peck if a woodpecker could peck wood... How much wood could a woodpecker could peck wood... How much wood could a woodpecker peck if a woodpecker could peck wood?"

"Very good," the woodpecker said, looking impressed. It flew up to the branch and got the key. "Now be safe, little one, and remember how much wood could a woodpecker peck if a woodpecker could peck wood!"

"Thank you!" cried Angelina. She ran to the door, placed the key into the keyhole, and twisted the wooden door knob. The door creaked open and the key magically disappeared out of her hand. With a flash of light it appeared back on the branch where it hung before.

Angelina began to walk down a spiralling stairway, taking each step with caution. When she reached the bottom of the stairway, she could not believe her eyes. She had arrived at a beautiful but very small village under the tree. It was full of tiny huts, some made of brick and some of straw.

"How bizarre," Angelina murmured.

Then she noticed something even more bizarre – the people who lived there were cats, and they walked on two feet just as they had in the fairy tale her father used to tell!

She looked around and saw a young cat, its fur as white as snow, picking blue berries. She excitedly walked up to cat and said, "Hello. Can you tell me where I am?"

"Oh my," said the cat, looking her up and down. "You must be a human. I haven't seen one of your sort before." And the cat walked all the way around her, studying her carefully. At last it smiled widely, held out its paw and shook Angelina's hand. "You are in Hollow Village. My name is Kitty. What is yours?"

Angelina, smiling back, replied, "I'm Angelina. Nice to meet you."

Kitty asked if she would like to see the village, and with great delight Angelina agreed. They walked upon the beautifully laid brick road and the first stop was the busy market place. They ran around the market place and got into all sorts of innocent trouble.

Kitty then took her to the see Grandma Milka, who was the oldest cat in the village: 504 years old to be precise. Grandma Milka was a cheery old cat who was very wrinkly but adorable nevertheless, and she always seemed to have a huge smile on her face. Grandma Milka sat the two down and told them one of her adventure stories from when she was a young kitten, gave them cookies and milk and sent them on their way.

Kitty had saved the best place for last, the Witch's forest, but before they entered the forest Angelina set eyes upon a black cat leaning upon a rock. Angelina asked who it was and Kitty replied that it was Mysterious Jack, and he very much kept to himself, and Kitty's mother always told her to stay away from him.

Mysterious Jack looked upon Angelina with an even more mysterious expression than before. After a while he slowly walked up to them and welcomed her to the village. Kitty was shy and didn't say anything, but Angelina began to talk to him. Kitty secretly nudged Angelina not to, but the little girl did not listen to the cat. Jack then asked them if they wanted to come along for a fishing trip. Kitty said they had to be getting home as it was nearly time for lunch. She tried to drag Angelina away. However, Angelina pleaded with Kitty that they go fishing with Jack. Kitty, not wanting to lose her new-found friend, agreed. So off they went to the lake where they had so much fun catching fish, laughing at all of Jack's funny stories that he told. It soon began to get quite late and the time had come to go home. Kitty warned Angelina on the way to her house not to tell her mother that they spent the day with Mysterious Jack.

Kitty's mother welcomed Angelina to their humble home with open arms and even gave her a room to sleep for the night. Later that evening when everyone was fast asleep and the night was young, Angelina was woken up by the sound of a knock at her window. She got out of bed and saw Mysterious Jack standing outside. Jack told her to sneak out because he needed her help, and without a single hesitation she did. Jack told her that they had to go and sneak into the Witch's hut and steal her wand. Angelina disagreed; as much as she loved adventures the idea of entering the Witch's hut scared her. Jack then pleaded with her that they had to, because the Witch had kidnapped his little sister and that was the only way to save her. Angelina, feeling very sorry for Jack, agreed to help him.

So the two went into the Witch's forest. It was darker than usual that night and deadly silent, which put a chill in Angelina's bones. They came to an old, grey hut with a big pointy roof, and Jack told her to sneak in through the open window. "Please," he said. "We must save my sister!"

Angelina hesitated at first but then seeing the desperate look upon Jack's face she gathered all her courage and climbed in through the window, trying not to make a sound. Once she was in the hut she crept around looking for the wand. The hut was full of many old spell books – some large, some small – and many cabinets full of potions. She then saw the Witch fast asleep on a wooden rocking chair, rocking backwards and forwards as she snored.

The Witch was hideous with a big pointy nose, messy grey hair and long, sharp, finger nails. On her lap was the wand. Angelina thought hard. Then, picking up a wooden spoon from a nearby table, she very slowly and carefully replaced the wand with the spoon. Taking the wand she quickly went to the window and jumped out. Jack, seeing her come out, whispered to her to come behind the tree where he was hiding. Angelina jumped up and down with joy for she had outsmarted a witch.

Jack suddenly snatched the wand out of her hand and rudely told Angelina to calm herself down. He let out a sinister laugh, and black smoke began to surround him. As Angelina watched in horror he transformed into an ugly, green goblin.

The goblin laughed. "The spell is broken!" he cried. "Now I will have my revenge!"

Angelina was confused and scared. Still laughing, Goblin Jack waved the wand at the trees, and they began to burn.

"No!" cried Angelina. But she couldn't stop him. Soon the whole forest was roaring in flames, and very quickly it spread to the village too. All the cats ran around panicking and meowing in fear.

"I must find Kitty," Angelina said to herself. "She will be in danger."

She ran out of the burning forest but quickly found herself lost within a crowd of panicking cats. "Kitty!" she cried, but her friend wasn't among the cats.

A thunder clap tore the air and a bright flash of lightning lit up the sky. Suddenly the Witch appeared and shouted, "You will pay for what you have done, Goblin Jack, to this beautiful village."

Goblin Jack began to laugh and asked the Witch what she could possibly do to him, for he had the wand. The Witch smiled cunningly and smashed a vial of potion on the floor. Tendrils of vapour curled up from the shattered glass and soon a fog covered the entire village. Goblin Jack could not see anything through the fog and he panicked. When the Witch smashed another vial of potion that created a shadow within the fog, Goblin Jack, thinking that the shadow was the Witch, began to hurl bolts of lightning from the wand. The Witch then threw a third vial of potion that created a swarm of bats that flew directly into Goblin Jack, taking him by surprise. The Witch quickly grabbed hold of her wand and shouted, "Elmarto Eldrio!" and everything in the village went back to normal and all the roaring flames were put out.

The Witch looked down upon Goblin Jack and he pleaded with her not to kill him. The Witch told him of course she will not kill him, as that would make her just like him, so instead she would turn him into a fish.

Goblin Jack screamed, "No!"

The Witch chanted a spell: "Fishy, withy, nippy, witty make this miserable goblin into a green fishy." And with a puff of green smoke, he transformed into a small green fish. The fish flip-flopped on the ground, flipping and flopping towards a nearby lake. The cats tried to catch the fish before it flopped into the lake, but it managed to flip-flop to safety before any of the cats could reach it.

The Witch then called upon Angelina, and she walked out from the crowd of cats with her head down in shame, walked up to the Witch and apologised for her actions. "I'm sorry," she said. "This is my fault. I thought you were an evil witch who had kidnapped Jack's sister."

The Witch, leaning down towards her, said, "Just because someone looks hideous it doesn't make them evil. And just because someone is beautiful doesn't make them good. What I am trying to tell you, little Angelina, is that you should never judge a book by its cover." The Witch then tapped her upon her head and said it was time she ought to get home, for her mother missed her very much.

"But my stepfather is horrible to me," Angelina said anxiously. "I'm safe here."

The Witch smiled. "I think you may find that your stepfather is no longer a problem," she said.

Angelina said her goodbyes to Kitty and everyone else and left Hollow Village. When she was back on the pathway to her home, the Woodpecker appeared, fluttered next to her and said, "So, Angelina, how much wood can a woodpecker peck if a woodpecker could peck wood?"

"I don't know," Angelina said, mystified.

The Woodpecker replied, "Until he pecks the nastiness out of it! You go home, and you'll know what I mean!"

Angelina ran back home as fast as she could, to find that her evil stepfather had been driven away from the house by a pecking woodpecker. Angelina looked up into the sky and thanked the Witch and the Woodpecker, and when her mother set eyes on her she gave her the biggest hug and the two lived happily ever after.

Spirit Chair

nce upon a time there lived a poor young man who was the village chair maker. One beautiful morning when he went into the forest to cut some wood he set eyes upon the most beautiful princess. The moment he saw her he fell desperately in love. He tried to speak to her, but she wouldn't even pay attention to him. Heartbroken, he went home and did not eat or sleep for days. Then it came to him if he could never be with her, he would at least send her something: a gift so beautiful that she will keep it forever. So he decided to make her the most beautiful chair she had ever seen.

The chair maker worked day and night for seven long days and on the eighth day he had finally finished the chair. It was magnificent – such detail, such craftsmanship – there was no chair within the lands as beautiful as this.

That night he felt he would sleep well for the first time since he'd laid eyes upon the princess, but a sudden flash of light filled his room and a spirit appeared to stand upon his bed. The spirit stated that it had come to make a proposition to him. "I've been watching you," the spirit said. I feel sorry for you that you love the Princess but she doesn't love you in return. I want to help."

"Thank you," said the chair maker.

"Don't thank me yet," said the spirit. Telling him there was no way that a humble chair maker could naturally be with a Princess, the spirit said that instead he would trap the chair maker inside the chair, and he would be with the Princess always. So the chair maker agreed without thinking about it twice, for he knew there was no other way he could be with the Princess. So as the spirit clicked its fingers and with a flash of black smoke the spirit made him one with the chair.

What the poor chair maker didn't know was that the spirit was, in fact, an evil spirit and had tricked him. By trapping him within the chair, the chair would allow any person who sat upon it to summon spirits from the other side, and on that day the spirit chair was created.

And so our story begins again hundreds of years later, when a selfish, miserable, power-hungry king heard about the spirit chair. He wanted it for himself, so that he could raise an army of spirits to conquer the world. The King found a map that would lead him to the chair, but it was coded, and he had not broken the code of the map. The King wrecked villages and killed many in search of the chair. Soon his Kingdom was in ruins because of his obsession to find the spirit chair.

Far in the east there was a small village close to the woods. One gloomy night soldiers were spotted riding towards the village and everyone knew what this meant: all their lives were in danger. A mother fearing for her newborn son's life wrapped the baby up in a warm blanket and began to run towards the woods. When she was shot down by one of the soldiers' arrows, the baby dropped and rolled into the forest and the riders did not spot it. The whole village was eventually burnt down and not a single soul was left alive.

That morning the sun rose as usual, and it was a beautiful day in the forest. The little baby boy began to cry as loud as it could. It cried and cried, the pitiful sounds echoing through the forest.

Finally something heard the baby's cries. A two-foot tall elf with long pointy ears and long skinny fingers climbed down from a tree. The Elf picked up the baby and was just wondering how to get rid of it – for it found the crying very annoying – when the baby stared up into the Elf's big frog-like eyes.

The Elf could not bring himself to get rid of the baby. Instead he took it up to his tree where he fed it some milk. The baby soon stopped crying and fell asleep.

The Elf was a lonely elf. His family had been eaten by the big, bad wolf and he was the only survivor. He had a scar on his back to show for it. Because he was lonely, the Elf decided to take care of the child as his own. He called the child Cole, for it had coal-black hair. The Elf grew very fond of Cole as he grew up and he even saw a great future for him, for elves can foresee destiny. The Elf decided to teach Cole everything he knew about the forest, animals and nature itself. The Elf even made a sword for him, trained him to use it well and taught him to hunt.

Years went on by and baby Cole grew up to be a handsome young man and a great hunter, in fact the best hunter to have ever lived. Cole was respected by the forest animals, for in time he defeated the big bad wolf that had destroyed many of the animals' families. Cole lived in a spacious wooden treehouse that the Elf had made for him within the same tree that the Elf lived. The treehouse was far at the top of the tree and had an amazing view of the beautiful forest.

One beautiful sunny day in the forest Cole went to cut some wood for the fire place. There he set eyes upon a beautiful maiden girl – she had beautiful sky-blue eyes and sparkling light brown hair. She was drinking water from the lake when she spotted Cole staring at her. She took hold of the little sword at her waist and demanded to know what he wanted.

Cole had never spoken to a human before, only elves and animals, so he didn't know what to say. His legs began to shake from nervousness and when she demanded he speak, Cole began to run as fast as he could. He climbed up his tree and locked himself in his treehouse. The Elf, hearing all the noise Cole made as he climbed up the tree, went up to see what was the matter. Cole told him everything that had happened when he saw the beautiful maiden. The little Elf laughed. "Fancy that," he said. 'The greatest hunter this forest has ever seen... a brave man like you... and you're afraid of a girl? That won't do. You must go and speak to her."

So Cole reluctantly agreed.

Cole spotted the maiden trying to pick an apple from a tree, but it was too high and she couldn't reach, even though she jumped and hopped and stretched her arm up. Cole saw this as his chance and quickly climbed the tree, picking the best apple he could find. He leaned down from the tree and held it out to her, not saying a single word.

The girl gazed up at him. "Can't you speak?" she asked. "Or are you just shy?"

Then a bird of the forest whistled for directions and Cole whistled back, helping the lost bird.

The girl was amazed. "Did that bird ask for directions?" she asked, and Cole nodded. "I've never met anyone who could talk to animals," she said in wonder.

Cole gathered the courage to speak to her and asked if she would like him to show her around the forest. Politely she agreed and told him that her name was Eleanor, and that day the two had a magnificent day. Cole showed Eleanor the wonders of the forest. He introduced Eleanor to his father the Elf. She told them that she lived in the forest but was far from home, and asked if she could stay with them for a while. They said yes.

Days passed. Then one dark night soldiers could be heard passing through the forest, which they had never done before, because it was the biggest forest in the land,

and they feared getting lost within it. Cole went off to find Eleanor, for she had gone to fetch some water. But as he drew near to the river, he heard the soldiers shouting. "There she is!" they bellowed. "We've found the princess. Capture her, men!"

Cole was astounded to hear that she was a princess, and knew she had lied to him. But even so, he knew he had to save her life. He rushed out, swinging his huge sword in one hand and a great wooden club in the other. The soldiers put up a weak fight and then ran away, leaving Eleanor and Cole by the river.

"Is it true?" Cole asked. "Are you a princess?"

Eleanor nodded. "I am," she said.

"So you lied to me."

"No," she said. "I didn't lie. I just didn't tell you who I was."

But Cole had been raised to believe that the truth was everything. He despised liars. "You must leave," he said. "I never want to see you again. And he turned and plunged into the forest.

Eleanor ran after him, explaining that she had not told him who she was so she wouldn't put his life in danger, because she had stolen the map for the spirit chair and her father the King was after her. But Cole would not come back.

The Elf jumped down from his tree and told Eleanor not to worry, that once Cole had calmed down, everything would be all right.

Two days later Cole was still not speaking to Eleanor. He did not utter a single word to her. The Elf explained that Cole was very stubborn by nature and to give him a little more time. Eleanor took out the map of the spirit chair and went to burn it, but the Elf saw it and knowing it was no ordinary map took it out of her hand. "What's this?" he whispered. An inscription was written on the map, which said 'No sooner spoken than broken'.

"A riddle!" the Elf said. He thought long and hard

about it and then finally shouted, "I've got it!"

"What?" asked Eleanor.

"I can't say," the Elf said gleefully. "The answer to this riddle is a secret."

Suddenly the map began to glow and all the drawings on it changed so the map became readable, and it showed that the chair was in the White Mountains. The Elf – who could see destiny – suddenly saw Cole's future. His destiny was to help the Princess find the spirit chair and destroy it!

The Elf brought the two together and told them that it was their fate to find the spirit chair and destroy it. Cole refused at first, but the Elf told him that he could not run away from his destiny. Eventually Cole agreed.

Cole and the Princess set out on their quest. They travelled across the west side of the forest taking a route towards the mountains, but Cole still being his stubborn self did not say anything to Eleanor. She tried hard to be patient but her patience soon ran out, and she screamed and shouted that she was sorry. "I should have told you I was a princess!" she exclaimed.

Cole suddenly pressed his hand across her mouth. "Be quiet!"

It was the first thing he said to her in days. She stared at him, her eyes wide. Cole looked around, curiously took a sniff and out from behind the trees came a huge, dirty, dark green revoltingly hideous crocodile with yellow glowing eyes. It snapped its huge jaws together and charged towards them, ready to bite into their flesh with enormous teeth like razors.

Cole quickly jumped from tree to tree to confuse the huge ugly crocodile until he managed to slash it across the neck. The crocodile fell to the ground with a loud thump. Eleanor thanked Cole, but he was still keen on keeping up with his stubborn behaviour. Not saying a single word to her, he then began to set up camp for the night.

What they didn't know was that the King's cunning spies had reported that the Princess and the Hunter were taking the route to the White Mountains, so the King knew that his daughter had cracked the riddle upon the map and that she was off to destroy the chair. The King and his soldiers were not too far behind.

Next morning Cole was up early while Eleanor was still fast asleep. He packed everything and woke her up by dropping her breakfast on her head – a single red apple. She angrily got up and followed him towards the White Mountain, and they began to climb it. They climbed for hours and hours. The King heard from his spies that the Princess and the Hunter were nearing the top of the mountain. He ordered his men that once they were at the top they must capture his daughter and kill the boy.

The Elf, meanwhile, had been watching them all along their journey by gazing into the forest rivers. He summoned lightning upon the mountain and a huge avalanche killed most of the King's army. The King, furious but determined not to give up, still carried on with the few soldiers he had left.

At long last, Cole and Eleanor made it to the top of the White Mountain and saw the entrance to their destination – the cave where the chair was hidden. However, before they could enter the dark cave, the King and his men attacked them. The soldiers shouted and swung their swords, but Cole was faster and more skilled, and Eleanor had her little sword too. The pair did battle with as many soldiers as they could... then suddenly, from within the cave's shadows, out walked a enormous six-eyed, eight-legged, hideous black-as-the-night spider. As the King's men began to battle the huge spider Eleanor and Cole slipped away into the cave...

And there it was, the spirit chair in all its glory. It was most definitely the most beautiful chair the two had ever set eyes upon. Cole walked up to the chair, about to destroy it, when in ran the King and tightly gripping his bow aimed an arrow at Cole. He was about to loose his arrow and kill the Hunter when Eleanor screamed and leapt in front of Cole.

The arrow pierced – not through the Hunter, but through the Princess's heart.

Eleanor fell into Cole's arms. "I love you," she whispered with her dying breath.

The King threw himself upon the spirit chair and began to summon his spirit army.

Cole gently laid Eleanor on the ground. "My love," he whispered.

Turning to the King, he angrily picked up his sword and drove it right through the King's heart, piercing through the spirit chair. The King died instantly.

Maddened by rage and grief, Cole quickly smashed the chair to pieces and set it alight. Then something magnificent happened from the flames of the chair: out flew the spirit of the chair maker.

"Thank you," the chair maker's spirit said, clasping Cole's hands in his own. "Thank you for freeing me. What can I do to show my gratitude?"

Cole bowed his head. "There's nothing I want," he said. "Not now that my love is dead."

But the chair maker's spirit had a gift to bestow – a most beautiful gift! He waved a spirit hand and suddenly Eleanor was standing right in front of Cole, very much alive. The ghost of the chair maker had brought her back to life.

"My Princess," said Cole.

"My Hunter," said Eleanor.

The two went home to their treehouse and were greeted with joy by the Elf. They married and lived happily ever after. Cole was never to act stubbornly again and Eleanor was never to tell a single lie.

The Lonely King

ong, long ago when witches cast curses and dragons flew among the kingdoms, there lived a young and beloved King, who lived in the shadow of his selfish and cold-hearted mother. The evil mother feared that once her son married, he would not listen to her any longer and might banish her from the castle. So one night she sneaked out of the castle and travelled to a Wizard's cave. There, she handed the Wizard a sack of red rubies.

"I want my son to always obey me and no one else," she said.

The Wizard cast a curse over the young King so that once midnight came, he would transform into a hideous green dragon. The Wizard told the evil mother to take the King to a cave every midnight and care for him until daylight when he would transform back to his normal self again. The Wizard also gave her a cursed dagger and told her that a small cut from this would kill anyone... but she should only use it when there was no other hope. Instead she should use love, because that is the most powerful magic.

Many years passed and there was talk among the villagers that there lived a furious dragon in the caves. They did not know that it was, in fact, their beloved King.

The King became fearful of himself and knew he was a danger to anyone around him during the hours of darkness. His evil mother liked him to think that way, as it kept him under her power. "I am the only one who can care for you," she told him. "You are a danger to anyone else. You must trust only me!"

One beautiful morning the King went riding on his horse through the forest. He came to a field at the end of the forest and decided to explore. Working in the fields was a young woman picking tomatoes. She saw the King on his horse and thinking he was a thief she began to shout and throw stones at him. One of them hit the King and he became furious. "How dare you attack the King?" he cried.

"I attack anyone who comes on my property," said the girl, tossing her long hair and flashing her wide eyes at him, "be they King or commoner."

This struck a chord with the King, for she treated him like ordinary folk which he desperately longed to be. He tried to talk to her, but she just told him to leave, and so he did. Once he went back to his castle all he could think about was that girl on the farm, her strong character, her beauty and how she treated him as if he was like everyone else, it made him feel normal which he had not felt in a long time.

Days passed, and the King could not stop thinking about the girl. He began to send her gifts to win her affections, but she refused everything he sent. "There must be something I can do to win her heart," he said. One morning the King secretly visited her and peeked through her cottage window. He saw that she was caring for her sick, dying father. So the King sent the best doctor in the entire Kingdom to cure her father, and the doctor cared seven days and seven nights for him, until he was fitter than ever.

The girl guessed that it had been the King who had cured her father, and she invited him for a meal that night. The King was heartbroken. He could not go anywhere at night because of the ungodly curse which was upon him. He wrote her a letter telling her that he would most definitely come for breakfast tomorrow morning but could not make it for dinner.

Next morning the King, very much excited, wore

his most beautiful and expensive clothes, he filled a chest full of gifts and went to the girl's cottage. Nervously he knocked on her door and when the girl opened it she was so delighted to see him and the King was delighted to see her. Before she invited him in, she immediately apologised for her previous behaviour. The King comforted her by saying that it was all in the past. That morning they both had the most delightful and joyous breakfast. It was as if the sun shone brighter that day and the birds sang for them. It was truly one of the most wonderful mornings both of them had experienced in a very long time.

That breakfast was only the first. Soon they met regularly. Every morning the King would go for breakfast at the girl's cottage and every morning his mother would ask him where he was going. He would reply that he was going for a swim. His mother soon began to suspect something, so she sent her black crow to spy upon her son. When the crow came back that afternoon and sat on her arm and the evil mother gazed into the crow's eyes, she saw everything the crow had seen that entire morning. She was furious to see the King had met a girl, and fearing he would make the girl queen the mother decided to get rid of her.

That night as her son transformed into a dragon, the evil mother broke the chains on him that kept him safely chained up, knowing that he would fly to the girl and hoping that he would end up killing her. So the hideous dragon that he had become flew into the night and terrorised the villagers, for he had no control of the dragon's beastly attributes. The King was not himself but a blood-thirsty monster. He flew to the cottage of the girl just as the evil mother predicted. The girl and her father were frightened and they tried to escape, but the dragon grabbed hold of the girl with its huge claws. It was about to gobble her up but then for a moment it stopped, and the father, taking his chance, stabbed it with a pitchfork.

The dragon let go of the girl as it blew out fire, roaring in agony. The King, taking control of his beastly form for the first time, controlled the rage boiling up within the beast and flew off into the night.

As the sun shone brightly over the Kingdom and the King was back to his normal form, his mother walked in to take care of her son's wounds. She saw that he was in a lot of pain, but most definitely not from his wounds. She asked him what was the matter and he replied that he had nearly killed the girl he loved and that he knew there was no way on earth he could ever love anyone, for he would put them in danger. "I must never see the girl again," he said. "If she comes here to the castle, please don't let her in, Mother. Never!"

With a devilish smile the evil mother agreed to her son's demands.

The girl awaited the arrival of the King that morning, and when he didn't arrive for their customary breakfast she began to worry. "Has he been hurt by the dragon?" she asked herself. She went to the castle walls, determined to see the King. The evil mother was waiting at the gates. She stopped the girl and said, "You cannot enter here," and told the girl her son did not want to see her. The girl refused to leave, so the evil mother took out the knife that the dark Wizard gave her and demanded she leave. The girl left, fearing for her life.

For many days in a row the girl walked to the castle and asked to see the King, but the evil mother had the guards to refuse to let her in. The girl, however, was not yet ready to give up on her love. This time she waited there from morning until night, and she saw the King ride out with his horse and the King's mother rode with him too. She followed them secretly into the dark forest and through the mountains into the dragon's cave, curious to know why the King and his mother had travelled here. Maybe she could get a moment alone with the King to speak to him?

The King and his mother sat within the cave waiting and as the sun began to set, the evil mother told her son that she was going to go get some water from lake, and that she won't be too long. After she left, the girl appeared in front of the King. "Why won't you see me?" she asked, tears in her eyes.

The King leapt to his feet. "What are you doing here?" he gasped. "It's not safe! You must leave now. Go on! Go!"

"I thought you loved me," the girl said. And as she looked into the King's eyes and saw the torment there she knew that he did love her. "Why can't we be together?" she asked.

"Please go…" the King begged.

And then it began. As the sun set and darkness spread across the land the King began to transform. Fearing for the girl's life he begged her again to leave, pushing her away as his skin slowly turned green and his fingers became claws.

The girl watched in horror. With a great flash of light that filled the entire cave the King transformed into a enormous green dragon. The girl was afraid at first and backed away. But she then remembered the look on the dragon's face when it attacked that night. She realised that he had been trying not to harm her. She gazed bravely up at the dragon and shouted, "I still love you."

At that moment the evil mother returned. She saw the girl and was furious. She pulled out the dagger the Wizard gave her and tightly gripping it slowly crept towards the girl, but just as she was about to stab the girl the dragon saw her and roared in anger. Breaking its chains, it grabbed hold of the girl and flew out into the night. The evil mother let out a furious scream of anger and, jumping onto her horse, rode off to the evil Wizard's hut.

The Wizard, busy creating potions, asked the evil

mother what she wanted. With her eyes sinisterly glowing in the candle light she took out the enchanted dagger he gave her, and stabbed the Wizard in the back. His lifeless body fell to the ground, killed by the evil weapon that he created. She picked up the Wizard's wand and shouted, "I will not be defeated. My son shall always obey me and no other." She waved the wand around and with a puff of smoke transformed into an enormous, hideous black dragon with fiery-red glowing eyes. She flapped her huge wings, and flew into the air, unleashing unholy fire from her mouth, setting fire to villages as she flew high up in the night sky.

The evil Black Dragon then saw her son flying through the air, gripping tightly to the girl he loved. Even though he was still in the beastly dragon form, somehow his love for her controlled the beast within him. Furious to see this, the evil mother let out a terrible roar. A huge burst of blazing flames issued from her mouth, engulfing her son. He dropped the girl, who fell down... down... down... into the forest where the canopy of tress broke her fall.

Overhead the two dragons began furiously to bite into each other, battling one another in the night sky. They bit into each other's wings and broke them, so they too fell into the forest with a great crash, but the trees did not save them. The  girl quickly ran to where they had fallen, fearing for the King's life, and saw both the dragons lying on the ground, gravely injured and dying. She ran to the dragon she knew to be the King, pleading for him not to die. The dragon turned its head slowly to her, gazed into her eyes and smiled. She then kissed the dragon

and with a flash of green light it turned back into the King
– the curse was broken by the power of love, for as the
Wizard had said, "That is the most powerful magic." The
greatly wounded Black Dragon saw this, slowly lifted her
head up to the moonlit night sky and let out one
last terrible roar as her bloody wounds killed
her. The evil mother was no more.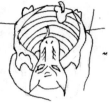

The people of the land rejoiced that
they would no longer live in fear of a dragon.

The girl tended to the King for many
months until all his wounds fully healed and
the two married and lived happily ever after.

Stone Princess

n a land far away, a Queen gave birth to twins, a Prince and a Princess. They were both loved dearly, but because the Prince was to be king, he was treated like a king and as they grew older the Princess's jealousy grew. Every day her jealousy got stronger towards her brother, until one day it turned into hate. The Princess had heard of a witch in the village, so she went to the Witch and asked how she could take the throne for herself. The Witch gave the Princess a magic brush and told her to brush the Prince's hair until it was as long as hers, then she gave her a small bottle of poison and told her to pour a bit in his wine and when he was dead, to cut her own hair just like the Prince's ,wear his clothes and dress the Prince in hers, to fool the castle that the Prince didn't die, but she had and so she could take his place.

The Princess went back to the castle and into the Prince's chamber, sat him down and took out the magic brush and began to brush the Prince's hair. Each time she did his hair grew longer and longer, she brushed his hair until it was as long as hers. Then she gave him a goblet of wine with the poison in it, and the Prince drank from it. Seconds later the Prince fell to the ground dead, so the Princess quickly dressed him in her clothes, and she dressed herself in his, also cutting her hair just like the Prince would wear his, and dragged the Prince to her own bedroom and laid him down upon her bed.

The next day the Queen found the lifeless body and – thinking it was the Princess who had passed away in her sleep – was distraught. The Royal Family placed the Princess within a royal stone coffin and sealed it shut. The Princess walked around the Kingdom dressed as the Prince and loved the new-found attention she had gained. The entire Kingdom thought she was the prince.

The Princess's ambition grew. She soon poisoned her father the King, finishing the entire vial of poison the Witch had given her. The Princess then became King of the Kingdom and ruled the lands with greed and hunger for more power. The villagers grew to hate the new King, for he would take all the best crops and always send his debt collectors every week to collect money, even from the poor. The once peaceful and rich Kingdom was now in poverty.

One day in the church a monk was dusting the royal tombs when he heard a thump from within one of them. He listened hard, heard it twice more and slowly pushed the heavy stone off a tomb coffin. Out leapt the Prince! He wasn't dead, for the Princess had made a mistake and not used enough poison. Instead the Prince had fallen into a deep death-like sleep.

The monk gasped in fear and, thinking it was a miracle, helped the Prince out of the tomb. "Oh, Princess," he said. "You're alive!"

"Princess?" said the Prince. Then he looked down at his clothes and, confused as to why he was in a dress, he shouted, "Bring me a mirror!"

The Prince looked at himself within the mirror. He saw his sister's reflection and not his own. "What is this?" he whispered, suspecting dark magic at play. He quickly picked up a blade and cut his hair, but it grew back again.

The monk, seeing this, guessed what must have happened and told him that he could only claim back the Kingdom with the help of the old Wizard Ozrak, who dwelled in the enchanted forest.

"Will you help me?" beseeched the Prince. "For I do

not know the way to the enchanted forest."

The loyal monk agreed to help him. "The Kingdom is in a terrible state," he said. "I will do anything to get the rightful King back on the throne."

Back in the castle the evil Princess-King was told 'he' had to marry so he could produce an heir. Being clever the evil Princess-King married a princess but four days after their wedding she lied to the castle guards that the new queen had tried to kill the King.

"She must be banished to a tower!" cried the evil Princess-King.

The poor wronged princess did not want to suffer imprisonment for a crime she did not commit and decided that the King had to be brought to justice. Sending word to all the villages that she wanted to bring justice back to the land, she raised an army – for the people wanted nothing better than to overthrow the evil King. They rescued the wronged princess from the tower, but as they prepared to march to the fake Princess-King's castle, the King heard about this and called upon the Witch to cast a most evil spell, turning all of them to stone to make an example of them. The wronged princess and her army were statues, all of them made of stone.

Meanwhile, the Prince and Monk had been travelling through the enchanted forest and had lost their way. The Monk was beginning to fear for their lives for he heard whoever entered the forest was never seen again, but then they heard a deep solid voice say, "What strangers do I see within my forest?"

They looked around but nobody was to be seen. They then heard the voice again this time telling them to look up. They looked up at the enormous tree to see its branches slowly lift up to reveal a face upon the trunk, and it said to them that it was the oldest tree in the entire world and asked what it was that they sought in the forest.

The Prince stated that they were looking for the Wizard Ozrak. The wise old tree then asked why they were seeking the old Wizard, and the Prince explained to the tree what had happened in the Kingdom. The tree hated injustice himself and told them he would aid them in their quest. The tree began to whistle and suddenly the trees within the forest began to move to the side to reveal a road.

The wise old tree told them to follow the marble road until they came to an old castle made of white marble itself. The Prince and Monk thanked the tree and carried on with their journey.

After walking for many days they finally arrived at the beautiful white marble castle. They entered the huge castle and set eyes upon an old, skinny, white-bearded wizard.

"I've been expecting you," the Wizard said. "Are you hungry?"

"Yes," replied the Prince and the Monk, for they had not eaten properly for days.

With a click of the Wizard's fingers, a massive feast appeared in front of them. After a delightful meal, the Prince was about to ask a question when the Wizard said, "I know what it is you want to ask, my young prince, and I must tell you now – you will not like the journey waiting for you. You must suffer to reclaim your throne!"

The Prince was prepared to do anything, so the Wizard agreed to help and told the young Prince that the only way he would overthrow the fake Princess-King was to break the curse of the stone princess and her rebellion army. The Prince asked how and the Wizard stated that first they would have to pass through the fire lake, defeat the black panther, then walk past the stone soldiers to find four statues of a stone princess. But only one was the real princess, and if he kissed the wrong one, he would turn into dust.

The Prince asked how he would know which one to kiss.

The Wizard replied, "Listen to your heart, boy, not

your head." And suddenly with a puff of white smoke the Wizard vanished.

So the Monk and the Prince began their quest towards the stone Princess's tower. The Prince and the Monk travelled for days through the enchanted forest until at long last they came to the roaring flames of the fire lake which the Wizard had spoken of. On the far side were black gates.

They had no idea how they were to cross the fiery lake, for they could not swim through it or they would burn. The Prince and the Monk sat down and wondered what they could use to cross the burning lake without it catching fire, for everything would burn within the roaring flames. A day passed and then the Prince spotted a huge boulder. He woke up the sleeping Monk to tell him that he had found how they could cross the lake. "Help me push the boulder into the lake," he said. "We can run across it to the other side."

They heaved and pushed and strained... and at last the boulder fell. They ran to the other side, flames licking at their heels.

They reached the black gates. Sensing danger, the Prince quickly drew his sword while the Monk held his trusty walking stick. They slowly walked towards the black gates. Behind the gate they could see hundreds of stone statues and right at the end, the four statues of the princess. Then suddenly a huge black panther with fiery red glowing eyes jumped in front of the two and let out a vicious roar, and the entire earth shook as it did. The Monk and Prince stood in fear, hearts racing, and they gazed at the enormous, black, blood-thirsty panther.

The Prince thought quickly. What could he do to defeat the panther? Suddenly he had an idea and shouted to the Monk, "Run to the burning lake as fast as you can!" and so they did. The panther charged after them, its huge paws shaking the ground.

Once they came close enough to the fiery lake, the Prince shouted to the Monk again: "Get down!" and as they ducked down the hideous panther went flying over their heads and into the burning lake. Unable to stop itself in time and burst into ashes.

The Prince and the Monk quickly ran past the statues of the rebellion army –there were hundreds of them, all stiff and white and stony. The Prince looked for a face that might be a wronged princess, but could see none. All of a sudden, with a puff of black smoke, the Witch appeared and with the flick of a wrist slammed them both to the ground. She was about to kill them both when suddenly a white mist formed around them and the Wizard Ozrak appeared, telling the evil Witch to leave while she could. The evil Witch let out a most devilish cackle, and the Wizard then demanded the Prince hurry and break the curse. As the Prince and the Monk ran past the many statues, the Wizard Ozrak and evil Witch began to battle between each other, summoning snow storms, hail stones, hurricanes and roaring thunders. The entire Earth began to shake as the two fought to the death.

The Wizard shouted out to the young Prince, "Listen to your heart, not your head!" and clapped his hands together. With a sudden burst of white light both the Witch and Wizard had turned to ice and had become frozen statues.

The Prince and the Monk at last came up to the four statues of the wronged princess. One was made of white marble, the other from clay, another from gems and one of the statues looked old and dirty as if it had been there for centuries. The Prince gazed at all of them and thought it must be the most beautiful statue, so went into kiss the one made of sparkling white gems. But before he kissed it, he thought it felt too easy. Looking at the old crumbling statue, and listening to his heart, he walked towards it and with a deep breath kissed the dusty stone.

Slowly the ground began to shake and the rest of the three princess statues blew up into dust, and suddenly the statues of the rebellion army began to crumble, and the villagers were once again alive. The curse was broken. The wronged princess thanked the Prince, and the rebellion army began to all march to the castle of the fake Princess-King.

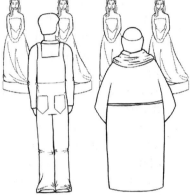

A bloody battle took place as they fought their way into the castle walls. The fake Princess-King was furious that his castle was being over taken by the rebellion army he had cursed.

The King began to pack up and abandon his castle when the Prince and Princess slammed the doors open and demanded the fake King stop. The Prince could not believe it. The King looked exactly like him. But when the Prince looked into the fake King's eyes he was heartbroken, for he knew those eyes. They were his sister's.

Hurt and betrayed by this he demanded to know why. She shouted that she was sick of always being treated as second best and that was to be no more. The fake Princess-King picked up the sword and charged towards the Prince and wronged princess. A furious fight took place as their mighty swords clashed, until the fake Princess-King was forced onto the floor by the wronged princess, for the Prince was reluctant to fight his sister.

The fake Princess-King was not going to give up, so she stabbed the Prince's leg and he fell to the floor. The fake Princess-King then disarmed the wronged princess and was about to kill her, when the Prince spotted the magic hair brush upon the table. He remembered it was the same brush his sister had used that night she tricked him, so he quickly picked it up and threw it into the fire place. It burst into flames. The spell was broken and they both turned back to their normal selves. The Prince demanded his sister see the error of her ways and pleaded with her to stop her madness, but with rage boiling up in her eyes, she ran towards the Prince to smite him down...

At that moment the Monk burst in through the doors. Picking up a sword on the floor, he flung it across the room and pierced the evil Princess though the heart. The battle was over. They had claimed back the Kingdom. The villagers cheered and the whole Kingdom was happy again. The happy day came when everyone celebrated, and the Prince was crowned king. He married the wronged princess and together they lived happily ever after.

Black Widow Queen

nce upon a time there lived a happy Kingdom, for the King and his family were happy and so were the people. The King had a beautiful wife, who he was very much in love with, and she gave him two sons and a daughter who he adored.

However, one dark winter the Queen fell desperately ill and passed away. The whole Kingdom was in mourning for their beloved Queen's death, except the Queen's evil sister Mandela. She did not even shed a single tear for her sister, for she had other plans. She tricked the King by being nice to him and helping him through the Queen's death. Soon the King married again. He married Mandela. Neither his sons nor his daughter were happy, because they knew their Aunt Mandela was a cruel person. Then another dreadful day struck the Kingdom. The King had passed away in his sleep. His people mourned for a long time except for Mandela who yet again did not shed a single tear.

The eldest prince claimed the throne, but Mandela was furious and sat in her dark, gloomy room stroking her pet tiger. She then whispered in his ear, "I will not have my sister's line of rats rule the Kingdom. The Kingdom shall be mine – all mine." And she began to cackle and as her evil laugh echoed through the tower. Even the creatures of the night got a cold shiver down their spines.

So Queen Mandela called upon her henchman, Cross-eyed Jack, who was mysteriously talented with the bow, even though he was cross-eyed. The evil Queen Mandela ordered him to capture and bring to her three venomous animals that could kill with just one bite: a snake, spider and the deadly scorpion. The evil Mandela patiently waited in her dark and gloomy tower for what she desired with all her black heart.

Three days passed and upon the night of the fourth day, Cross-eyed Jack entered the dark, gloomy tower where Mandela and her tiger waited patiently. When he walked in Mandela was sat stroking her tiger as it purred with delight. As Cross-eyed Jack placed the three sealed boxes upon the table, Mandela's evil coal-black eyes glowed with joy. One box contained the deadly cobra, in the other was the lethal scorpion and within the last was the venomous black widow spider. Mandela screamed in delight and with great joy, she shouted, "Tonight shall be the end of my sister's line, and I shall be queen forever!"

And so she took the three baskets, jumped on to her black horse and made her way to the castle. First she crept into the young King's room, opened the basket and the black widow spider slowly crept up his body and with a single bite, the poor young King let out his last breath. Without wasting any time she crept into the young Prince's room and opened the second basket, and out crept the scorpion, which wasted no time and stung him with its venomous tail, so the poor prince, just like his brother, was also killed. The devilish Mandela then crept into the beautiful Princess's room, opened the basket and the cobra slithered out into her bed, but Mandela was shocked to find that the bed was empty. The door opened and the Princess entered and asked in confusion what her aunt was doing there. Mandela lied and pretended that she had just come to check up upon her and told her to go back to sleep. As she slowly pulled up her covers the hideous snake suddenly popped out his head and hissed a horrid hiss, ready to bite. The Princess screamed in fear and jumped away from the bed, and falling backwards, tripped over her stool and fell out of her window. The evil Mandela then let out her evil crackle with great delight.

However, what the evil Mandela did not know was that the Princess had fallen on to a stack of hay, and she was still alive. The scared Princess quickly ran into the nearby barn and hid in fear among the cows, and cried herself to sleep that horrid night.

The next day as the sun rose and the word of the death of the Royal Family spread through the Kingdom, everyone was in mourning yet again, except Mandela, who now sat on the throne. The entire palace suspected that she had murdered them all, but were too afraid to say or do anything, for fear of what she might do to them. Among the Kingdom she became known as the Black Widow Queen, who with her venom poisoned the entire Royal Family.

Meanwhile, a young stable boy entered the stable to go about his duties just like he did every day. He picked up a bucket and went to milk the cows when to his shock he set eyes upon a beautiful girl. Mesmerised by her beauty and innocence, he just stood and stared at her. She then slowly opened her eyes and when she set eyes on him, she screamed and cried, "Please don't hurt me."

The boy then calming her down told her that he wasn't going to hurt her, and she had no reason to fear him. Not telling him that she was the Princess and lying to him that she was a servant girl, the young man said to her that she was the most beautiful servant girl he ever saw. Blushing at the flattering way he talked, she sat and listened to him, thinking what a nice voice he had and that she could listen to him talk for days on end.

Meanwhile back in the castle the Black Widow Queen Mandela was feeding her tiger fresh meat, when her henchman Cross-eyed Jack burst through the doors in a panic and said he could not find the body of the

Princess anywhere. The evil Queen Mandela screamed, "What?!" and slammed her feet on the floor with fury. Stating that a dead girl could not get up and walk away, she told him to go and find her body, stating he had until nightfall or her tiger would feast on his flesh. To ensure that he did not run away, he was to take her pet tiger with him.

Back in the stables, the stable boy and the Princess had been talking for a long time, when suddenly a scruffy, furry, brown and very cute dog jumped onto the Princess and began to lick her. She screamed at first but then begins to giggle as it tickled her. The stable boy dragged the dog off her and told her that she had now met his best friend, Scruffy. Then the stable boy's father shouted from outside, telling him to go and pick some berries for his mother as she had run out of berries for the blueberry pie. So the stable boy, the Princess and Scruffy head off into the woods. However, what they didn't know was that Cross-eyed Jack and the Black Widow Queen's tiger were not far behind.

As the Princess picked blueberries the stable boy just could not stop looking at her – he was mesmerised by her, and the Princess knew he was looking, but she was trying to act as if she didn't know. Then suddenly they heard a twig snap and they all stood still when Scruffy stared at a bush and began to bark. They hear a terrible tiger's roar which made Scruffy stop barking, and the three began to run as fast as their feet could take them. From the bushes Cross-eyed Jack and the roaring tiger appeared, but instead of running after them Cross-eye Jack climbed up a tree and aimed his trusty bow at the running Princess. The Princess stopped running for she had come to the edge of a waterfall. Cross-eyed Jack loosed his arrow and pierced her in the back. She fell off the edge of the waterfall so the stable boy quickly jumped after her and so did Scruffy. The boy caught her in mid-air and they fell into the river with a big splash. Scruffy quickly dragged them out of the river and they both lay unconscious on the ground. Scruffy licked their faces to wake them up but it was no use. A shadow of a tall hunchback figure appeared, Scruffy began to growl so the figure pointed at Scruffy and he fell asleep.

Many hours later the stable boy woke up in an old wooden hut full of skulls and bones of animals. He was very cold, so he ran to the fireplace and tried to light the fire, but the wood would not catch. Then suddenly the flames burst to life by themselves. The front door creaked open and the stable boy picked up a rod and gripped hold of it tightly, fearing who was about to enter. In walked a tall and very skinny grandma with a huge hunchback, long grey hair and wearing gypsy-like clothes. She then assured him that there was no need to be afraid of her and asked him to follow her into the next room, which was where the Princess was sleeping. Scruffy was sat by her bed side, hoping she would wake up. The stable boy turned to the gypsy and asked if she was dead. The gypsy told him that she was asleep, not dead, but soon to pass on over. The stable boy began to cry and dropped by the bedside. The gypsy slowly pulled him up and asked him if he loved the girl. The stable boy replied yes without any hesitation.

"Very well then," said the gypsy. "There is a way to save her – an impossible one but yet a way." She told him that up the fire mountain lived a dragon, and if he could get a single drop of his blood it would heal all her wounds, for dragons' blood had magical qualities. So the gypsy quickly rummaged through a wooden chest, handed him a sword and blessed him before he and Scruffy left.

Meanwhile back at the castle the Black Widow Queen had just received the news from Cross-eyed Jack that he had killed the Princess. The evil Queen was full of joy and decided to celebrate with a huge feast. She ordered her chef to cook the most wonderful feast that he would ever cook, or she would have his head.

Meanwhile, out in the wild, night had fallen. The stable boy and Scruffy had been climbing for hours and had finally come to the entrance of the fiery mountain where the great Dragon dwelled. They entered the cave slowly, not making a single sound, when they came across the huge snow-white Dragon which was fast asleep and blowing out fire each time it snored. The stable boy slowly pulled his sword out, gripping it tightly, and went in to cut through the Dragon's scaly skin to take a drop of blood. But as soon as the sword touched the Dragon's snow-white, glistening skin, its head sprung up and it roared a terrible roar, and a great burst of fire shot out of its mouth.

Scruffy and the stable boy quickly ran round the cave as the Dragon snapped its teeth, trying to swallow them whole. Scruffy bravely jumped into the air and began to scratch the Dragon's eyes out, until the Dragon was blinded. It roared in agony and smacked poor Scruffy with its enormous tail. Scruffy fell to the ground. The stable boy – horrified to see his little dog treated so badly – picked up the sword and sliced the Dragon's head clean off. The Dragon's huge body fell to one side as its head fell to the other. The stable boy quickly took out a vial and filled it up with the Dragon's blood and ran to leave the cave, calling Scruffy's name, but Scruffy did not come or make a single sound. He laid on the floor very much still. The stable boy ran to his dog, making him drink the blood of the Dragon. He waited and waited but nothing happened, for Scruffy had already been dead for some time. The stable boy shed a tear for his old friend and wished him farewell, for he knew he had to hurry back if he was to save his love.

The stable boy picked up an old burnt shield he saw

on the floor, sat on it and pushed himself off the edge of the mountain, screaming his lungs out as he slid down and crashed into the gypsy's front room. She quickly took the vial of Dragon blood and dabbed a drop on the Princess's lips, and they wait and wait and wait. When she slowly opened her eyes and jumped into the stable boy's arms and gave him a kiss, the gypsy watched in happiness. Then the Princess asked where Scruffy was. The stable boy told her what happened to poor old Scruffy. But suddenly a miracle happened and they heard Scruffy's bark. They all ran outside and could not believe their eyes – Scruffy had grown. He was enormous! Almost twenty foot tall! He was as big as the Dragon and had also grown massive dragon-like wings too, but was still very much a dog. He bent down and licked them all with his huge tongue. The stable boy turned to the gypsy and asked how it was possible.

"Anything is possible with dragon's blood," said the gypsy. She then turned to the Princess and said to her it was time to reclaim her Kingdom.

"Your Kingdom?" asked the stable boy. "What does she mean?"

The Princess turned to the stable boy and told him who she really was. He couldn't believe his ears. The three quickly jumped on Scruffy's back, and they flew off into the sky as Scruffy flapped his huge new-found wings.

In the mean time, the evil Black Widow Queen was celebrating with Cross-eyed Jack and her mean tiger. She walked out onto the balcony of the great castle, talking about how she would conquer the entire world. "Everyone will fear and worship me like a god!" she cried. But Cross-eyed Jack pointed into the sky and shouted that there was a huge flying dog. The Black Widow Queen turned around and could not believe her eyes.

From afar, the gypsy lifted up her hand and began to chant something which went a little like this: "From air I summon it within, to burn strong of will and smite down the untrue and burn the soul for all." This summoned a huge bolt of fire and it went flying into the balcony. The Black Widow Queen screamed for the last time as she and Cross-eyed Jack and her tiger were all turned to dust.

The Princess reclaimed her beautiful Kingdom, married the stable boy and they lived happily ever after.

The Music Box

nce upon a time in a faraway kingdom when magic was alive and well, there lived a princess so beautiful that her beauty was known throughout the lands. She had fiery red hair and lips as red as a rose, with mesmerising sea-blue eyes. She was known thought the Kingdom as the Angelic Princess. Many travelled from across the land to seek her hand in marriage, but her beloved father adored her so much and cared for her like no other, that he never thought any of the princes were fit to marry his daughter.

One day war had hit the lands and the King being a wise king knew wars cost money, so he decided to get rid of some of the luxuries around the castle. He called upon the gypsy fortune teller Trina, who was a young woman with dark coal-black hair and a sinister beauty about her. She bowed before the King as she entered his study.

"Trina," said the King. "I regret to inform you that your services are no longer required."

Trina, shocked, said, "I beg you to reconsider, your Majesty."

But the King stuck to his word. Trina was furious and refused to leave. The King called upon his guards to escort her out, and as they dragged her Trina screamed at the King, "Mark my words, King, with the dark arts invested in me I will make you pay!"

Trina, thrown out of the castle like rubbish, shut herself within an old, crumbling stone hut where she was most definitely up to no good. She sat reading through spell book after spell book, to find the most evil spell to cast upon the King. And then it came to her: why cast a spell upon him when she could cast a spell on his most beloved possession, his beautiful daughter the Angelic Princess. That was what Trina would do. She lifted her hands up above her head and chanted a most evil spell which went a little like this:

Up and down, side to side, I summon a melody so fine, it dulls the senses and traps the mind, as the notes play two by two, it drains your youth and beauty too, birds fly high and so will death, one two three I trap the melody simply within a box like thee.

And with a flash of black smoke, a music box appeared upon the wooden table, the first music box to ever be made. Picking it up the evil Trina grinned, devilishly proud of her wicked spell. Transforming herself into a black crow, she flew to the Angelic Princess's chambers and placed the music box upon her table.

The next morning the Angelic Princess was woken by the sparkling diamonds upon the music box on her table. As she opened the music box a melody began to play. The Princess was charmed, for the melody was a fine one. But as each note played, she began to grow older and older, until she caught a glimpse of her reflection in the mirror. She was horrified to see her once beautiful self had been turned into a old horrid hag! Distressed, she shut the music box. What would people say when they saw her, she wondered? What would her dear father say? He was so proud of her beauty... he would be revolted by the way she looked now.

Terrified, the Princess ran away, far away from the Kingdom and settled down within an abandoned cottage in the forest. Her only friends were the animals which dwelled in the forest. She cleaned and redecorated the cottage but made sure to get rid of every single mirror, accept one which she kept tightly locked up within a cupboard. She brought it out every New Year's Eve to take a look at her reflection, hoping the curse would be broken. But every year she would let out a most terrible scream that would send a cold shiver through the animals of the forest.

Meanwhile Trina crept into the castle and stole back the music box so that no one would ever know what she had done. The King searched high and low for his lovely daughter. Many years passed but he never gave up hope. He ordered his soldiers to search for her every single day. One night when the stars shined brighter than ever, the Angelic Princess heard somebody scream for help. She ran towards the voice to find that the young blacksmith of the next village was trapped in his burning cottage. Acting quickly she and her trusty animals quickly put out the fire, and she pulled him out of the burning cottage. As he opened his eyes, a star began to shine down upon her and her old hag look withered away to reveal her once beautiful self. The handsome blacksmith, mesmerised by her beauty, gazed at her like nobody had gazed in a very long time. She ran to a puddle to take a look at her reflection to see if the curse really could have finally been broken, but when her reflection revealed her hideous old hag appearance, she let out a terrible scream, ran back to her cottage and cried herself to sleep that night.

The young blacksmith, not being able to think of anything else but the beautiful maiden who had saved his life, decided he would look for her. He knocked on every villager's door but all told him that they had never seen a maiden as fair as he described. After many days of searching, he then came to the cottage within the forest and could not believe it when he set eyes upon the Angelic Princess picking strawberries from her farm.

He said to her, "I have not been able to stop thinking about your fiery red hair and rose-red lips since the day you saved my life."

The cursed Princess replied, "The fiery red hair you talk of is as white as snow and the rose-red lips you speak of are as pink as flesh… it's a cruel joke you play upon an old hag." And she demanded he left at once.

Confused and refusing to leave, he took her hands, gazed into her eyes and pleaded to her that he was not playing a joke. "You are lovely," he said. "I see no hag."

Seeing the way he looked at her made her feel beautiful and young again as she once was, so the Angelic Princess told him about the curse that was cast upon her many years ago. The young blacksmith, very much in love, assured her that he would find a way to break the curse and end her suffering.

So the adventure began. The blacksmith set out on his journey, but that day the sun shone brighter than usual, making it harder for anyone to ride. The young blacksmith stopped by a lake to take a sip of water when he heard someone pleading for help. Tightly gripping hold of his sword he witnessed a poor young boy being pushed around and laughed at by two cruel soldiers. The blacksmith quickly and swiftly disarmed the soldiers and driving them off helped the boy up. But to his shock the boy was no child but a little dwarf, with a long, ginger beard and big shiny eyes.

"Thank you," said the Dwarf. "I owe you my life."

He asked where the blacksmith was off to and if there is anything he the humble Dwarf could help with. So the blacksmith explained everything to the young dwarf. The Dwarf smiled and told him he was meant to save him, for the blacksmith was in luck. The young dwarf's mother was a user of magic, and she could most definitely help him upon his quest. So the two travelled to Dwarf Mountain. The blacksmith could not believe his eyes when he entered the mountain, for there was an entire kingdom within it. It was a most beautifully built kingdom – its houses, chapels and markets were mesmerising to gaze upon.

As they entered Mother Dwarf's hut, she had already poured them some dwarf tea, which smelt a lot like boiled grass, which made the blacksmith feel a little sick. Mother Dwarf said she was expecting the two and taking out an axe she cut a rock in half and began to read it like a rune. Mother Dwarf told the young blacksmith that the only way he could free the Angelic Princess was to break the curse on the music box. The Mother Dwarf, quickly rummaging through her drawers, brought out a white crystal. As it lay in the gnarled palm of her hand it began to glow white. She told the blacksmith that when the crystal glowed white like this, it meant he was in the presence of a user of white magic, but when it glowed red then it meant he was in the presence of a user of black magic. She told him to use it to find Trina. She also gave him an enchanted sword to help him upon his quest, and sent the blacksmith and dwarf on their way.

The two travelled for days and became good friends on the journey. Eventually they made it to the walls of the Kingdom. Near the castle they stopped for food in a tavern and while the Dwarf began to eat all the meat and chicken he could scoff down his little mouth, the blacksmith kept a watchful eye upon the crystal in case at any moment it glowed red.

A woman in black robes passed by their table. Her arm brushed against the blacksmith and to his amazement, the crystal began to glow red. "Quickly," said the blacksmith as he watched her leave the tavern. "We must go after her!" Dragging out the Dwarf as he was biting into a big piece of chicken, the two follow the woman. She made her way to an old hut. The blacksmith drew his sword and the Dwarf his axe and they burst into the hut. But the woman wasn't there.

"What shall we do?" asked the Dwarf.

"We look for the music box," said the blacksmith.

"But what does it look like?" asked the Dwarf.

Before the blacksmith could reply, six statues within the room magically came to life and began to attack them. Fighting their way through the brave pair saw an open trap door. "One... two... three!" cried the blacksmith, and on three, they jumped in, slammed it shut, and fell into a dark, gloomy tunnel.

The blacksmith took out the bright red glowing crystal which lit up the tunnel. To their horror, the light also revealed a swarm of hideous green goblins which began to attack them. Slashing and cutting their way through they finally enter a enormous hall full of all sorts of creepy things, and there, sat upon her chair, was Trina stroking her ugly pet lizard, Balthazar.

"What are you doing in my chamber?" she snapped, her eyes flashing.

"I've come for the music box," said the blacksmith, trying to sound brave, although inside he was full of fear for he could tell she was evil.

Trina let out an evil cackle, and her lizard sneered. "What on earth do you want with the music box?" she asked.

"I'm here to break the curse you've put on the Princess," the blacksmith said, his voice ringing out strong and true.

Trina cackled again and said that nobody would ever break the curse until the end of her days. "Eat them, Balthazar," she ordered her lizard.

The hideous lizard charged towards them but with a single strike with his enchanted blade the blacksmith killed it. Trina screamed in rage and anger, hurling bolts of lightning at the two. She then stopped and began staring at the Dwarf and the blacksmith with her piercing eyes, and let out another evil cackle like before. Chains began to wrap around the two and tied them up against a wall, and she told them that she would leave them here to rot.

The Dwarf had a trick up his sleeve though... he began to whistle and two moles popped up from underground.

He asked them to seek help from the old hag in the cottage, who was actually a princess. The moles began to dig as fast as they could and when they found the Princess, they told her that the Dwarf and blacksmith were captured by the evil gypsy Trina and needed her help.

The Angelic Princess leapt onto her trusty horse. "Ride like the wind," she said.

Soon she was at Trina's hut and, seeing the trap door, went down it. She bravely passed the bloody corpses of the goblins and at last found the blacksmith and the Dwarf. Picking up the enchanted sword she set them free.

"How dare you!" screeched Trina. "I will summon snow storms, hurricanes and all means of dark magic to defeat you!"

But before she could so much as utter a spell, the Dwarf leapt on to Trina. She lost her balance and fell backwards, hitting her head on a rock so that she was killed instantly. Out from her pocket fell the cursed music box. The Princess saw it and rushed over. She stamped on it many times, breaking it into millions of pieces, and with a bright flash of light the curse was broken and her old hag look withered away.

The Angelic Princess and blacksmith married, and the Dwarf was their best man at the wedding, so proud in his peacock-blue suit. After their enchanting wedding, the three lived happily ever after.

The Serpent Ring

nce upon a time in a faraway land there lived a young king. As the King was very young he never took on his duties as King seriously but instead enjoyed the luxuries of being a king and wreaking havoc around the castle. His uncle, who always lusted to be king, was jealous of his nephew and it angered him to see the way he did not take his duty as king seriously.

One day, as the young King played around in the garden picking apples from the trees and tossing them at the soldiers around the castle, he accidently hit his uncle on the head. Fuming with rage his uncle went to grab the boy, but the guards got in his way. Going back to his tower and consumed by his hatred even more for the young King, his uncle sold his soul... and the Serpent Ring was created.

The young King was in the library reading his favourite book when in walked his uncle smiling sinisterly. He told the young King to come and sit upon his lap, for he had a gift for him. As the young King sat on his lap the uncle passed him a little brown wooden box. The young King opened it very excitedly and set eyes upon the Serpent Ring. Waiting for something more exciting he closed the box and did not wear it, but the uncle then said to him that it was a magic ring, and so the young King quickly opened the box and placed the ring upon his finger. With a flash of green light that covered his body, he fell unconscious into his uncle's arms. His uncle laughed with great happiness and then shouted for the guards. They came rushing in to find the King lying upon the chair, not moving. They quickly took the young boy to his room and the castle doctor came to take a look at him but could not figure out what was wrong with the king. He was very much alive but it seemed he had been poisoned by something which had sent him into a deep sleep. So the Kingdom was left with no king and next in line to rule over the people was, of course, the uncle.

For many years the uncle ruled with great power, expanding the Kingdom greatly and winning many battles. The people came to love him, for he bought great wealth to the Kingdom. The young King was still asleep after many years and cared for within his tower by a maiden. Then came the day when the Kingdom was attacked by an even more power hungry and ruthless king, and the entire castle fell apart, except for the tower in which the young King slept. Many years passed on by and tales began to be told of the long lost King who slept within the tower, waiting to be awoken. After hundreds of years, many battles took place in the great Kingdom with many kings claiming the throne. The day came when the Kingdom was left without a king, and many argued about who would be the next ruler. The Kingdom was in devastation of civil war.

One day out of the ashes of war rose a Phoenix who said, "From the ashes of this Kingdom how I have risen, and so will your king. For he sleeps within a tower where your Kingdom's castle once dwelled and you must find him before there is nothing of your Kingdom left to fight for."

Many army generals came and discussed this, but most agreed not to wake the King and fight until one of them was king, for if he slept for this long who knows what he will do when he is awakened. But one caring general disagreed and tried to convince them that this was the only way for peace, but none of the other generals agreed and so secretly taking his army he went in search of the tower where the King slept. He travelled far and high, but they were soon lost. The Phoenix then appeared to them from the flames of their camp fire and told them to cross the Red Sea and they shall find the tower in which their king slept and that they must break the curse upon him by the Serpent Ring.

So the Caring General and his army, not wasting any time, began to build a ship and within a week they were ready to sail. As they sailed through the calm blue sea, sometimes the winds looked to be on their side, until one day the winds were still and they could not sail, and the boat floated within the middle of the sea as they rested for the night. Suddenly they could hear the most enchanting singing voice, and then they began to hear many enchanting voices, singing to the soldiers. They all looked down the side of the ship and there were many mermaids gathered around, singing to them. Then the mermaids began to call them in and soldiers began to jump into the sea one by one, for they could not control themselves – it was like the enchanting song had taken control of them, and soon all the soldiers were dragged deep under the sea, never to be seen again.

Thankfully the Caring General was a heavy sleeper and did not hear the evil mermaids sing. He woke up to find his ship empty and no sign of his soldiers, but to his astonishment he spotted a centuries-old tower which looked as if it was going to fall apart any minute. He quickly got off his ship and stepped on to land, and began to walk around the old tower looking for a door to enter, but there was none to be seen, except for a window far up in the tower. So taking his bow out and tying a rope at the end of his arrow fired it onto the roof of the tower and began to climb up. He entered a dusty room filled with vines, leaves and spiders' webs. He then spotted the young King lying asleep upon his bed, who had not aged a day. The General ran to the bedside and began to look to see if there was a serpent upon him that the Phoenix spoke of, but there seemed to be no snake. The General then spotted the silver Serpent Ring upon the boy's finger.

He slowly pulled it off and with a flash of green light the curse was broken and the young King slowly opened his eyes after hundreds of years.

All of a sudden the fire place lit up and from the flames of the fire appeared the Phoenix who thanked the General and said to him that it only takes one person to make a change. The General then told the Phoenix that his army had vanished, but the Phoenix stated that they had not vanished but been taken by evil mermaids. Comforting the General and telling him not to worry, the Phoenix said that the General would be able to make the other Generals listen.

The young King and the General jumped on to the Phoenix's back and soared though the beautiful clear blue sky until they came to the boy's Kingdom which was in a state of destruction, engulfed in flames and reduced to rubble. The Phoenix let out a roar that echoed though out the Kingdom, and getting all the generals' attention he told them all to listen to him, that here was their new king and it was time to end the fighting. One of the generals boldly stepped forward and stated that he would never take orders from a boy and went to strike the young King down. The Phoenix stared at him with its yellow eyes and they began to glow red as the roaring flames around them and the general burst into flames. The other generals, fearing for their lives all bowed down to their new king.

The boy was crowned king once more and the Caring General who had broken his curse became his most trusted advisor… and they lived happily ever after.

Magic Perfume

nce upon a time within a faraway Kingdom there lived two sisters. One of the sisters had hair as blonde as the glowing sun, skin as fair as silk, with eyes as blue as the sea. She was called Aurora. The other sister envied Aurora, because she herself did not possess such beauty – she had messy black hair, frog-like eyes and was quite fat, for she enjoyed her food... possibly a little too much. She was called Gilda. Every year the All Hallows Eve ball took place and all the men of the Kingdom would fight for Aurora's attention, but not a single man would even glance at the ugly sister, Gilda.

The envy and jealousy Gilda possessed for her sister grew stronger by the year. One year as the ball approached, she decided she'd had enough, and she wanted to be the centre of attention at the All Hallows Eve ball. And so jumping on her trusty horse, who was in fact her only true friend, Gilda went riding to the tower of the village alchemist, who with science and magic brewed all sorts of potions.

Gilda walked up the spiralling stairs to enter a room with many shelves and cabinets full of hundreds of potions of all shapes and sizes. In walked an old man with a long, white beard that dragged across the floor, and he was gripping tightly on his walking stick. When he looked at her she screamed with fright to see that he had no eyes. She could even see a glimpse of his brain through the holes where his eyes should be. He demanded to know what she sought from him. Gilda, trying not to look at his face for it gave her the cold shivers, told him that this All Hallows

Eve ball she wanted all the men to fall in love with her and not her sister. The old man sinisterly smiled and told her that he had just the thing for her, and walking up to one of his cabinets, pulled out a perfume vial. Gently pulling out a piece of her hair he dropped it into the vial, and it began to bubble up. He then handed it to her, telling her to spray a little of it on and any man would fall in love with her as soon as the scent hit their nose.

As she went back to her home, Gilda could hear her sister shouting at her servants to hurry up and get her ready for the ball. The ugly sister smiled joyfully as she walked past her sister. Her sister turned around and mockingly asked her why she was smiling so joyfully, had she eaten all the pies for the all Hallows Eve Ball, and began to laugh. Griping tightly to her perfume vial the alchemist had given her, the ugly sister told her that tonight she would have the last laugh and walked to her room. She began to happily get ready, humming her favourite song as she did.

Night had fallen and everyone left for the ball except her. As Aurora entered the ball, all the men immediately began to ask for a dance. Later that night Gilda's carriage pulled up by the palace, and before she got out, she began to spray the magic perfume upon herself. Forgetting that the alchemist told her only to spray a little she instead had sprayed the entire vial on herself and tossed the empty bottle out of the carriage window.

When Gilda entered the hall and the scent of her perfume hit the noses of the men, they were all instantly mesmerised by her and ran towards her to ask her for a dance. Left all alone at the other side of the hall, Aurora was hurt and – not knowing what was going on – began to cry. Gilda was having the best night of her life, dancing with different men and being treated like a queen. For once she knew how her sister felt every time she went to a ball. She saw Aurora crying and felt a secret pride that she was now the centre of attention and Aurora was not. "Now you know how I feel at every ball, sister," she said.

Aurora sniffed into her silk handkerchief. "I'm so sorry, Gilda… I never realised. I can see now how much it must have hurt you to be left alone at every ball." She reached for Gilda's hand. "You must have felt so lonely."

Meanwhile, all the men began to fight for their love for Gilda. They had gone mad with love and could not bear to share her. They all drew their swords and began to battle each other. She pleaded that they stop, but none of them listened to her. A bloody battle took place, and she watched in horror as all the men began to kill one another, until none of them where left alive. Gilda burst into tears. "Oh," she wailed. "What have I done?"

Aurora looked puzzled. "What do you mean… what have you done?"

Gilda told her that she had gone to the alchemist and he had given her a magic perfume that would make everyone fall in love with her, but she was only supposed to spray a little of the perfume and instead she sprayed the entire vial on herself! Aurora took her sister's hand and told her they had to go to the alchemist and ask him to reverse what he had done. Together they hurried out of the palace. As the soldiers guarding the gates got the scent of Gilda's perfume, they began to shout and chase after her. The two sisters ran through the village as the soldiers, under a mad love spell, chased after them. They finally came to the tower of the village alchemist, and quickly running up the spiralling stairs they slammed the door shut and tightly locked it behind them.

The alchemist was there sat upon his wooden chair waiting. The sisters demanded that he reverse the potion's effects.

The old man smiled, but it was not a nice smile. "Yes

of course," he said. But you must pay me."

Gilda quickly stated that money was not a problem. The old man let out an evil laugh and said money was not what he wanted, but her eyes.

The sisters clung together with fear, and asked if there was nothing else he wanted.

"No!" the alchemist cried. "I want nothing but your eyes! I need your eyes." And he gestured to his own empty sockets.

Suddenly Aurora spotted a big toad jumping about and whispered to Gilda that she had an idea. She leaned close and quickly shared her plan. As the soldiers banged on the door trying to break it down, Gilda went after the toad. She said to the alchemist, "You can have my eyes, but you must reverse the spell now, or the soldiers are going to break the door down."

The alchemist then asked how she will guarantee to give him her eyes, so Gilda handed him the key of the door. "I give you my word," she said.

The alchemist thrust his hand into the pocket of his robe, took out a vial, and smashed it upon the floor. The room filled with smoke and as the smoke faded away, the soldiers all stopped banging on the door. The alchemist impatiently demanded her eyes, so Aurora told him that she would cut out her sister's eyes. The alchemist nodded as he waited eagerly for Gilda's eyes.

Gilda pretended to scream in pain while her sister cut out the toad's eyes. Aurora handed the eyes of the toad to the alchemist, and as he placed each eye in his empty sockets, the sisters wait in fear. When he opened his eyes he let out an evil laugh and shouted, "I can see again!"

But suddenly his eyes began to burn up and he screamed with agony and demanded to know what was happening. The sisters told him that they were, in fact, toad eyes. The alchemist screamed in despair and pain as he began to burn up. He burst into roaring flames and with a sudden bang turned into dust.

From that day on Gilda never envied her beautiful sister again, and Aurora always spent time with her sister at all the balls they attended, never leaving her alone, and they lived happily ever after.

The Chatty Prince

ack, far back, in the mists of time when the world was very young there lived a young handsome prince who always seemed to talk and talk, so he became known throughout the Kingdom as the Chatty Prince. People began to hate the young, handsome prince for he would always be talking and talking about this and that, and how he knew everything.

One day an old hag entered the castle and asked the Prince if there was anything he did not know, and the Prince said that there was nothing he did not know, for he knew everything. He began to talk and talk about how he knew this and that, and nobody could tell him differently. The old hag, tired of the Prince's talking, lifted up her hands and began to sway them side to side. She started to chant something, which went a little like this:

Chitter-chatter, bitter, batter, turn this prince into what chitter chatters.

Suddenly the Prince transformed into a parrot. The old hag placed the Prince in a cage and sold him at the market. The Parrot Prince pleaded with its owner to let him go, for he was actually a prince and had to break the curse that the old hag had cast upon him. However, the owner laughed and found the parrot to be very amusing, thinking that it was the Prince. The Parrot Prince still went on talking and talking until he was put up for sale at the market again, for the owner was fed up of all its chitter-chatter. The Prince went through many owners, all finding the parrot amusing at first, but soon after realising that it never kept quiet, they subsequently went on to sell the bird.

One day an old, lonely granny bought the parrot, but this old granny definitely talked more than the parrot did. Every day the granny would talk and talk until she fell fast asleep. The Parrot Prince realised that this was indeed what he sounded like, and seeing that the granny lived all alone with no friends and family made him think that he most definitely did not want to end up like her. So he vowed never to talk again. The granny, thinking the bird was sick and that was the reason why it was not talking anymore, sold it to a Princess in the market. When the Parrot Prince set eyes upon the beautiful Princess he was struck by her beauty. He wanted to talk to her but he had vowed never to speak again, and he was intent in keeping his vow, for he knew it must be the only way to break the curse. Days went on by and every morning as the Princess fed the parrot and stroked its head, his love grew for her. It made the Parrot Prince think about his past life how many beautiful princesses he must have driven away from all his talking.

One day when the Princess left to eat supper, the old hag entered her room where she kept her parrot and said to the Parrot Prince, "I have been watching you and see that you have been learning about the error of your ways." The Parrot Prince quickly nodded yes, and the old hag went on to say, "Now here is your next task. You are only allowed to utter one single word every day, and if you can get the Princess to free you, then you shall transform back to yourself."

The parrot nodded in agreement and so when the Princess entered her room the Parrot Prince uttered his one single word, which was "Listen." The Princess went to listen and the parrot uttered the word again, "Listen" but when the Princess waited for the parrot to say something else, it only repeated the same word, "Listen."

The next morning the Parrot Prince said a different word: "Freedom." He kept on uttering the word "freedom" repeatedly. The Princess asked the parrot if he was not happy in his cage. The parrot shook its head, signalling no and he kept on shouting, "Freedom!" The Princess, feeling sorry for the parrot, agreed to set him free. When she opened up the cage to free the parrot, the Prince couldn't help himself and shouted, "I love you." With a burst of light he transformed back into a prince again.

The Princess was shocked to see her parrot gone but a handsome prince standing in its place. The Prince sat her down and began to listen to her talk... and from that they on the Prince never spoke as much as he did again. He always listened to what others had to say before he began to speak, and when he became king he was beloved by all his people for his understanding nature and the way he would listen to anyone, no matter who they were, and so he lived happily ever after.

Enchanted Chest

nce upon a time within a faraway Kingdom there lived an adventurous king. One day as he went on one of his quests with his trusted soldiers they found a chest within a cave. They tried to open the chest, but it was no use. They tried to smash the chest open with their swords, but it seemed to be enchanted and nothing could break through it. The King was intrigued by it and decided to bring it back to his castle to investigate how to open it, for he knew since it was highly enchanted there must be something wondrous within it. So for years he tried and tried but nothing seemed to open the chest.

Within one of the villages of the Kingdom lived a young poor boy and every morning he woke up and stared at the castle in which the King lived. The young boy always dreamed of having a castle of his own, but he was not as fortunate as the King, for his family were very poor. The boy went into town one day to pickpocket some food for his family when he was caught by one of the King's soldiers. The boy begged for them to let him go and vowed that he would never steal again, but they never listened to him. Instead they took him to be punished he was brought inside the castle walls to have his hand cut off for stealing. The boy acted quickly and stamped on a soldier's foot, ran into the castle and looked for a place to hide. He quickly tried all the doors within the castle corridor, but they all seemed to be locked. Finally he found one of the doors was unlocked, and pushing it open he quickly entered the room and slammed the door shut. He began to look around the magnificent room, which was full of beautiful things he had never even set eyes upon before: golden plates, diamonds on goblets and huge, beautiful paintings upon the walls. Then his attention was grabbed by a chest: curious to see what was in it, the boy slowly walked up to it and crouching down on his knees, he turned the circular golden knob upon the chest and it clicked open. When he lifted the lid up it revealed the many rubies that were within the chest all in different shapes and sizes. They glittered in the sunlight as the boy picked up as many as he could. He started to put some in his pockets when suddenly in ran the guards to arrest him.

But when the soldiers set eyes on the enchanted chest, they realised that it had finally been opened after all these years. They quickly summoned the King, and as he entered the room, he could not believe his eyes. The chest had finally been opened. The King dipped his hands into the many glittering rubies within the chest, but as he picked one up, it turned to dust and the chest slammed shut again. The King tried to open the chest, but it would not budge as it had sealed itself shut. He called the boy to open the chest again just as he did before, and so the boy did as the King said and as he twisted the circular golden knob the chest opened again. But when the King went to pick up the rubies from the chest yet again they turned into dust, and the chest sealed itself shut. The King furiously stated that he would not allow some street brat to take his chest and demanded to know how he was doing it. The boy, very much afraid of the King, nervously told him that he did not know. So the King demanded that he opened the chest again, but this time to take all the rubies out of the chest and place them upon the table. So the boy fearing for his life did exactly what the King said and emptied the chest full of rubies onto the table. As the King stared at the glittering rubies he was mesmerised by them and he went to pick up one, but they all turned into dust and went flying back into the chest, which slammed shut and tightly sealed itself. The King was enraged and boiling up with anger grabbed hold of the boy and demanded to know how he was doing it, but the boy did not know – it was like the chest had chosen him and not the King.

The King then demanded the boy to open the chest again and so he did, slowly twisting the golden knob, and as it clicked, the chest flung open but this time all the rubies began to magically fly out of the chest and began to join one by one, as if a jigsaw, to form a dragon made of glittering rubies. The soldiers and King backed away in fear.

The Ruby Dragon stamped its huge feet as it walked up to the King and said, "This chest may only reveal its wonders to those who really need it and not to anyone else."

The King nervously said to the Ruby Dragon that he had found the chest. Suddenly the Ruby Dragon angrily began to stamp its huge feet on the ground and as the ground shook it said, "Nothing in this chest belonged to you, nothing! Everything within the chest belongs to the boy for he has been chosen."

The boy grinned with delight and could not believe the chest had chosen him. So he jumped onto the Ruby Dragon, and flew out of the castle. They went soaring through the sky and the Ruby Dragon glittered even more brightly as the sun shinned upon it. As the Ruby Dragon landed in front of their crumbling wooden hut, the Ruby Dragon began to fall apart and turned back into hundreds of pieces of rubies in all shapes and sizes. The boy's whole family could not believe their eyes as they came outside the hut, as hundreds of rubies were lying in front of their door.

And so the boy built a magnificent castle for himself and his family from the many rubies he possessed and lived happily ever after.

The Wishing Well

eyond the woods, beyond the seas, beyond high mountains, in a faraway Kingdom there lived three princes. The three brothers always loved to mess around their father's Kingdom and one day as they went exploring the youngest Prince saw a well. He was very intrigued by it and went to look what was inside, but when the young Prince leaned too far forward into the well he fell in.

His brothers, hearing his scream, went to help their little brother and climbing down the well using a rope, they realised it led to a cave and they found him crouched up in a corner crying his little eyes out. When he saw his brothers he jumped up with joy but when they went to climb back up the rope they found it had vanished. With no way of getting out the three brothers began to walk deep into the cave to see if they could find another way out. As they kept walking deeper and deeper into the cave they began to get quite tired. Suddenly they heard a cackling sound and it sounded a lot like a witch's cackle. The three brothers drew their swords gripped hold of them very tightly as they waited in fear. Then up above them three Witches flew in on their broomsticks. When they spotted the three princes they stopped in mid-air, hovering above them. The first Witch had a tall and skinny body with a pointy long nose and long grey black hair; the second Witch had snow-white hair, with a pale white face and pink fleshy lips; and the third Witch was quite fat, you could tell she loved her food, and she had bushy grey hair and reptilian eyes.

The first Witch stared at the princes intensely and asked

if they were lost. The eldest Prince stated that it was none of their business and to be on their way. The second Witch's eyes widened and said, "How rude you are, young man."

The second Prince whispered to his brother that maybe they should seek the witches help, for they could see there was no way out after travelling deep into the cave, so the three princes, being quite tired and missing their warm cosy beds, turned to the Witches and apologised. They went on to say that yes, in fact, they were lost. The third Witch smiled and mockingly said how unfortunate, licking her big fat lips, as if she was hungry and the princes were to be her next meal. The first Witch gave her a slap around the head and told her to hold her wicked tongue. So she offered to fly the princes out of the well, for a price. The eldest Prince asked what the price was and the Witch said she could not think of one at this moment in time. However, she was sure to have thought of one by the time they flew them out of the well. So the eldest Prince and second Prince agreed, but the youngest, being quite frightened of the Witches, did not agree. His brothers comforted him saying that there was nothing to worry about and reluctantly he agreed.

The eldest jumped on to the back of the first Witch's broom, the second oldest Prince jumped on the second Witch's broom, and the youngest Prince hesitantly jumped on the back of the third Witch's broom. The Witches let out another spine-tingling cackle and told the princes to hold on tight, as they began flying through the cave.

They flew out of the well and placed the princes back on land. The princes were so happy to be out of the dark gloomy well and hugged each other, and forgetting about the Witches price they joyfully jumped around.

Then all three Witches loudly coughed to get their attention.

The three princes turned to the Witches and the eldest

asked what the price was for their freedom. The Witches sinisterly smiled: the youngest Prince, they stated. The eldest and second eldest prince quickly drew their swords and pushing the youngest Prince behind them demanded the Witches leave, for there was no way they could have their little brother. The Witches began to cackle and the first Witch stated that they really had no choice and were powerless against them.

The three Witches took out their wands and began to chant a curse:

Black as coal, black as night. Summon a black mist to cloud the night.

Suddenly a black mist formed around the princes and as the mist slowly vanished, the eldest and second eldest prince heard their little brother's voice from within the well, crying out for help that the Witches had taken him. The two princes, fearing for their brother's life quickly jumped down the well to save him but there was no sign of the Witches nor their brother. And so they began to travel down the cave and walked and walked, not stopping to rest for a moment, for they knew their brother was in danger.

Meanwhile back at the Witches' hut within the cave the Witches had tied the young Prince up and the first Witch began to go through her spell books looking for a most evil spell. When she found it she called her sisters to gather around.

This is what it said within the book:

To gain one's youth one will need certain things; first you will need six fresh toad

119

legs, two unicorn horns, eight tears of a baby, a monkey
head and the last and the most vital ingredient: the
heart of a young prince.

The other two sisters quickly went rummaging through their cabinets. One witch shouted excitedly that they had six fresh toad legs, the other shouted that they had the monkey head and a vial of baby tears, but the other witch, taking out one unicorn horn from a jar, quite upset by this, stated that they were missing a unicorn horn. So the first Witch told the two to go and fetch one, as she would begin to make the potion, but as she looked for fire wood, there was none to be seen. Taking out her wand, she said they had no choice but to use their magic broom sticks as fire wood. The other two sisters cried no, but the first Witch said there was no time to lose and pointed her wand at the three broom sticks lying on the floor. They hovered across the room and she snapped them in half, placing them under the cauldron and they began to burn. The other two sisters screamed in devastation but the first Witch quite angrily demanded the two to stop their whining and to fetch another unicorn horn, so the two sisters left the hut slamming the door behind them.

Meanwhile after the two princes had been walking for some time, they came to an enormous bridge. They were just about to cross it when suddenly it began to shake, and as it did it lifted up into the air to reveal a huge troll. They had mistaken it for a bridge. The Troll with its deep voice stated what did they seek on the other side. The eldest Prince told the Troll to let them pass, for they had to find the Witches hut and save their younger brother. The Troll then said that the Witches hut was, in fact, not on the over side, but down the river. The princes not seeing a boat to cross the river with asked how they would cross it. The Troll began to dig into its huge pockets and pulled out a rowing boat, placing it on the river; he said that they could cross the river with it if they bought him back a pig. And so the princes agreed and jumping on to the boat began to row and row.

They rowed for many hours until at long last they spotted a tall stone hut with a large roof. Knowing this must be the Witches' hut they quickly got out of the boat and began to sneak towards the hut. When suddenly they heard the Witches cackling, they quickly hid behind a wall. Then they saw the second and third witch walking towards the hut, tightly holding on to a unicorn horn, and as they were about to enter the hut the two princes quietly crept behind them and cut off their heads. Taking their long black robes, they quickly slipped them on and covered their faces with the robes' long pointy hood, and picking up the unicorn horn they walked into the hut, making sure the first Witch did not catch a glimpse of their faces. She demanded they hand over the unicorn horn, and so they did.

The Witch cut up the unicorn horn, placed it into the boiling cauldron and began to chant, "Bubble, bubble, boil and steam, as I place the ingredients within a potion like thee, I summon the fumes to bind and bloom to form my potion to grant my youth." Suddenly, with a big bang green smoke began to steam out of the cauldron, and she shouted to the others to cut out the young Prince's heart and bring it to her.

The eldest Prince nodded and

making sure the Witch did not see his face he walked up to his younger brother. He struggled to escape but the eldest Prince revealed his face and whispered to his little brother that they were here to save him. The Witch then screamed at the two: "What's taking you so long?"

The second Prince then spotted a jar of pig's hearts. He quickly took one and passed it to the Witch, who is too busy mixing her potion to notice what they are doing. Tossing it in, she began to cackle in delight. Pouring the potion into a wooden goblet, she began to drink, and as she did her skin began to bubble up. She screamed, and with a puff of smoke, she was transformed into a pig. Squealing like a pig she tried to run away, but the princes quickly caught her, tied her up and placed her upon their boat. They begin to row towards the troll and when the troll demanded his pig, they handed over the pig-like Witch. The troll quickly gobbled her up.

"Can you help us leave the well?" asked the princes.

"Not I," said the troll. "The only way of leaving this well is by flying."

"But the witches burned the brooms! What are we to do?" The princes began to panic but the troll remembered that witches always keep special brooms hidden in case they ever need to escape. They rowed the boat back to the hut. The troll jumped off and discovered the brooms in the back of a cabinet stacked with jars full of potions and the hearts of innocent animals.

The troll ran back to the boat and tossed a broom to each of the princes. They leapt upon them, balancing carefully, and flew around and around… and then up and up… and finally they flew home. There, they lived happily ever after and they never went near the well again.

Christmas Fairy

nce upon a time there was a poor family in Victorian London. They lived in a small worn down house. There was a mother and father and their three sons and daughter and they all worked night and day so they could bring food upon their table. The mother cleaned other people's houses, the father worked within one of the great factories and the children sold the beautiful flowers their mother would grow within their garden. However, winter was the worst for them, for their house was never warm enough from not having enough fire wood to light the fire, and food was always more scarce then usual. This was because the children could not work in the winter as their mother's flowers would die in winter.

However, even after all this the children always loved the winter, for they played within the snow making snowmen and snow angels, and they always excitedly awaited the arrival of Christmas Day, because for them it was the best day of the year. Every Christmas Eve their father would leave early to head off to the market and find a turkey big enough and cheap enough for their family. But, as he got to the market place this particular Christmas Eve all the turkeys had gone as well as the chicken too and the meat was too expensive for him to buy. The father was devastated for he did not want to spoil his children's favourite day of the year. So the father travelled all across London on that cold winter's day, searching through every market place he could find, but every market seemed to be sold out of turkeys and chicken. He walked to the edge of the forest and was already covered in ice, for he had been searching for hours on such a cold winter's day, but his last hope was to cross through the forest to the market at the far end. But suddenly, just as he started, a massive pile of snow fell on top of him, and he couldn't escape.

Meanwhile, the children at home excitedly awaited the arrival of their father, but the sun set and as the moon shone across London there was still no sign of him. The children began to worry and so did the mother too. It saddened her so much to see her children's devastated faces on Christmas Eve, which was a time for joy and celebration, and she couldn't bare to see their Christmas cheer vanish, so she sat them round and told them all their favourite stories and played with them until they fell fast asleep. The mother lit a lantern and went out to look for her husband on that very cold night, but although she searched and searched around the village and town square, there seemed to be no sign of him anywhere – it was as if he had vanished.

Christmas Day had come and the children ran down the stairs, even more excited and joyful than ever, for they were to see their father and open their presents. But they came down to find their mother had just spoken to police at the door, and as she shut the door, she sat down and began to cry. The children gathered around their mother asking where their father was. Their mother quickly wiped away her tears and said that their father had gone away for a while and would not be here for Christmas, but they could still go ahead and open their presents anyway. The children refused and sat down by the fire and decided they were to wait for their father. No matter how much their mother pleaded with them to open their presents, for she knew very well that their father was not to return, they still would not open them. Night fell, and it was time for the

Christmas dinner and all they had was mashed potatoes and peas on their plates, for that was all the mother could find. The children refused to eat without their father and stayed seated by the fire place, determined to wait.

As the fire and candles burned they waited and waited. Without warning the windows slammed open as a gust of wind blew into the house, blowing out all the candles and the fire too. It was pitch black and they could not see anything at all. The children began to panic and shiver as the cold took over their house.

But then something magical happened: the room began to get warmer and warmer as it had never been before. The windows slam shut and hundreds of floating candles lit up the room. The children looked up at the beautiful floating candles in such amazement and their mother did too. Then they set eyes upon a most beautiful Christmas tree, glittering with tinsel and all kinds of decorations, and under the tree it was full of expensively wrapped presents. Then all of a sudden there was a knock at the door...

The mother and children ran to the door and opened it, and to their amazement, standing before them was their father. The children jumped into their father's arms with such joy, and the mother gave him a kiss upon the cheek as they walked in to their warm and cosy home. The father was cold and his coat was wet, and the family fussed around him as they heard how the snow had fallen on him. "How did you get out of the snow?" asked the mother. And the father said he did not know, but that he felt sure the spirit of Christmas had looked after him.

The whole family then set eyes upon the most magnificent feast laid on a beautifully decorated table. There was a huge turkey – the biggest turkey they had ever seen – and chicken, lamb, potatoes, pork chops, cookies, cupcakes and even a Christmas pudding. All the candles began to slowly glow bright and brighter until they were glowing so bright the family had to shut their eyes. When they opened them, hovering above the magnificent feast was a tiny little fairy no bigger than their fingers, dressed in red and white. She wished them all a happy Christmas and told them that this was her Christmas present to them from her, for she had seen what the father went through just to keep his children's Christmas spirit going, and had also appreciated their understanding of Christmas.

"There is no Christmas without the ones you keep dear to your heart," she said with a smile.

The whole family thanked the fairy and invited her to join them at their Christmas feast. She kindly accepted. The fairy then clicked her fingers and grew as tall as their mother. Now she was big enough to sit upon the empty chair at the table. They rejoiced and all had the best Christmas Day with their entire family, for what was Christmas without the ones you loved?

The End

Acknowledgements

With thanks to all the people who have helped make this
book a reality:
My mother, father, sister and grandparents
My family in Cyprus
All my friends in Bristol
And all my friends and family in London

I thank you all from the bottom of my heart for all your
support. I could not have done it without any of you.

Thanks to Gina Alice Purnell for her editing.

Also great thanks to my illustrators:
Kirsty Ogden
Somiya Nagem
Kiranjeet Kaur
Annabel Horsefield

Lightning Source UK Ltd.
Milton Keynes UK
UKOW051148270412

191600UK00001B/5/P